FRIENDLY TIES

Leslie L. Daniels

authorHOUSE®

AuthorHouse™
1663 Liberty Drive
Bloomington, IN 47403
www.authorhouse.com
Phone: 1 (800) 839-8640

Published by AuthorHouse 05/19/2017

ISBN: 978-1-5246-9158-5 (sc)
ISBN: 978-1-5246-9157-8 (e)

I would like to dedicate this book to all my friends and family who believed in me and gave me the courage to get off my butt and send in my story for publication. I also want to say a special thank you to those who inspired me and brought my characters to life.

Blessed Be! Peace, Love, and Light!

Prologue

Elements is a witch with wicked fighting skills and always fighting the battle between good and evil. She deals with white magick and black magick, super natural bad guys as well as human bad guys. It is no wonder she gets called the ultimate weapon. She deals with powers that seem out of this world and in some cases, they are.

She also must deal with shape-shifters and psychic vampires that want her dead. This is nothing compared to the battle she must fight within her heart. A lover from her past has resurfaced again after leaving without a trace or a goodbye. She must try and keep the balance between good and evil, as well as keeping her friends alive. With the help of her friends and some unlikely allies will this be enough to win and keep her heart, or is it a losing battle from the start?

CHAPTER 1

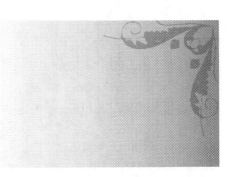

I T WAS A GORGEOUS DAY; the sun was shining and if the wind caught you just right you could smell the ocean. Florida is like that. Just about anywhere outside you can smell the saltwater of the ocean, but sometimes early in the morning it smells like fish but you get used to it. There are so many things I would love to be doing on a day like this but sadly that is not the case today. Instead of laying out on a beach, or sitting in the park relaxing, I am running down a dirty alley way chasing some asshole.

It smells like old food because the sun was beating down on the trash cans and dumpsters and that makes it very unpleasant to the nose. It is so over powering in some areas that you must breathe through your mouth just to keep from vomiting. The garbage that has been thrown out from various restaurants on both sides of the alley was getting baked from being in the sun. My eyes are watering so much that it kind of feels like I just cut up an onion.

I look at the ground so I can watch where I'm running and to make sure I didn't step in any of the animal feces on the ground. There are so many stray cats running these allies looking for food and that's not even counting the wild animals like raccoons, possums, and skunks. I am also having to watch out for broken beer bottles and dirty needles that are scattered about, left by the hookers and drug addicts that frequent the alley ways at night.

This was the part of the job I hated. The running. I always said that if I wanted to run I would have taken up jogging. It never fails, whenever you go after bad guys they always run down alleys. It's not just in the movies. In real life, they're that stupid. I turn and look over my shoulder

1

because I could hear my partner running behind me. She was panting trying to keep up with us.

"Behind the third dumpster Elements!" Christine yells.

I look forward and can see the B.B. U's foot sticking out. That is short for Big Bad Ugly. I also know that he is about to throw some serious magick my way. I hit the ground in a tuck and roll and yell a reversal spell to counter act his. The next thing you hear is a loud, "Boom!", and the B.B is gone, erupting into blue flames.

Christine reaches my side and asks through gasps of air, "So the son of a bitch go up in flames?"

"Yup, and it was oh so pretty. "Sarcasm just dripping from my voice as I look over at her and wink.

We stand up straight and we both head back to the car walking very, very slowly. No matter how many times you must run after assholes like him in the job your body never gets used to it. Christine shares my same opinion about running, she hates it too.

I walk over to the passenger side of the car and get in, while Christine gets in the driver's side. I close my eyes and lean back in the seat and command my body to not stiffen up on the ride home. Everything I saw starts replaying in my mind. I turn my head towards the window so I can feel the sun on my face. Even though it's hot, the heat felt good to me. It meant that we had survived another take down. *Can I get a Yee-Haw?*

Christine starts the car and turns to me, "You alright Elements?"

I look at her through slit eyes and see the sun reflecting off her hair. It looks like a burgundy fire and the ends were getting burnt because her tips are dyed black. I love her hair. She is the only one I know that can pull that look off. If it were on anyone else, it would just look like they had a fight with the dye bottle and lost but on her it just looked cool. I was paying my price for magick, a headache was forming and the sun was just intensifying the pain. You see when you use magick you pay a price and mine was the onset of a migraine.

"Yeah, I'm fine just a little headache. How are you doing?" I ask her.

"Well I feel like my heart is about to beat right out of my chest and my feet are killing me. Did I ever mention how much I hate to run?" We both start laughing as she puts the car in drive.

"Ditto my friend. As for your feet, no one told you to go running in thigh highs." As I look at her leather three-inch heel boots.

"Hey, I paid two hundred dollars for these I'll be damned if I'm not going to wear them, besides they look so cute with this outfit." I start laughing so hard tears form in my eyes. *She knows her priorities.*

Christine is what the metaphysical world call a sensitive. She can feel magick and when it's being done. She can also distinguish whether it's black magick or white. That makes her a great asset to any team. I can't really tell the difference magick is magick. At least not until the end. In our line of work that can be very hazardous to someone's health preferably not mine.

Christine and I have been working together for about three years. In those three years, we have taken out some major bad asses in the magickal world. It is not just us though we have one more in our little family and that is our friend Detective Jay with the police. He has his own little skill and that is his stubbornness which has gotten him out of more jams then his freakin gun ever could. The man does not give up for anything because that is a sign of weakness and we all know a man cannot show weakness. At least in his eyes.

Jay has only been working with us for about a year in a half. That is only because he witnessed one of our so-called take downs and we needed his help to keep the law off our asses. He was like, *Sweet! Can I play?* And that was all she wrote. Since then he has become a very dear friend to the both of us.

Since the three of us have joined forces we have been able to stay one step ahead of the bad guys. They aren't too far behind though we can feel them nipping on our heels. Jay helps us with some of our cases and in return we help him with some of his.

CHAPTER 2

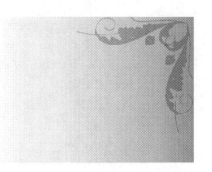

W E ARRIVE AT MY HOUSE which is small but comfortable. It used to be my grandparents but when they passed away they left it to me. I was their only grandchild so I got spoiled. I look at the house and have a flash back and see my smiling grandparents sitting on the porch and I'm drawing on the sidewalk in front with my chalk. I do talk to them every once in a while, but the Divine don't like you bugging the dead to much so I have limited it to Halloween and maybe a few other times throughout the year.

My house is Headquarters for my business. The Super Natural Squad. It's a small three bedrooms, two bathrooms, and a study with all the other normal stuff in a house. The kitchen is my favorite part though. To me it is very retro. I like the black and white tile floor and red appliances. It kind of reminds me of an old fifties diner. It is single level and made of brick. It has two huge trees on either side of the house so it helps keep the house cool in the summertime, and in Florida that is a blessing. Not to mention it helps keep my power bill down.

I try and make my house as normal as possible, so I planted some flowers in a small garden and put a bird feeder out in the yard. My flowers die and the squirrels steal the bird food so I guess that's normal. Goddess knows I don't need any extra attention drawn to me. I already know some of my neighbors wonder about me slipping in and out at all hours of the day and night. It wouldn't be a surprise to me if some of them thought I was a prostitute. I have never been big on what others think of me. I say let them think whatever the hell they want. The less they know the less I have to explain, so needless to say I don't get invited to any barbeques.

There a lot of people out there who are happy and content in their own little world. The thought of witches, psychics, and cops who help chase magickal creatures just do not fit in to their beliefs. Ignorance is bliss they say and that's fine with me. You know brunettes who want to be blondes don't fit into my beliefs but I don't bitch about it. Let's just say it's a give and take thing. I get rid of big bad ugly and give protection to those who need it, and I get peace and quiet because I don't have to shoot the breeze with nosy ass neighbors. It is a beautiful relationship.

I walk through the front door and I'm ecstatic I have no stairs to climb, except for the three steps to get onto the porch to the front door. The way my body feels right now I couldn't do stairs even if I had help.

I formed the S.N.S about five years ago after I tangled with a major bad ass and almost lost. All though he has been underground ever since I still look over my shoulder thinking he's going to pop up and try to finish what he started. The only thing I worry about are his lynch men. His bullies on a leash as I call them. All though the longer he stays underground the more powerful he becomes.

I lean against the stove with the phone to my ear waiting for Jay to pick up. As I listen to the ringing my legs begin to shake because of all the running I did. My body still is not use to that. It's sad.

"Talk to me".

"Hey Jay, its Elements."

"What's up?"

"Just wanted to let you know that Christine and I took out that pain in the butt, he's gone" Just some new vamp that was trying out his powers and ended up hurting some people. If they mind control you for too long you can forget who you are which is what happened in his case. The victim was a minor and now she's in the loony bin because she just rambles on making no sense.

"I wish I was there. It would have been more exciting than my morning. "He says with a little envy in his voice.

"Yeah, I know Jay but you have your work and we have ours. Plus, if the shit ever hits the fan you will be free and clear. You can play ignorant and still have a job. You understand"?

"What are you my mom? Slow your broomstick, I understand. "He says now annoyed with me.

He's not really upset he just hates the fact that I'm right. Christine starts to laugh because she can hear Jay and what he's saying. I can't help but to start to laugh as well because her laughter is infectious. When she laughs it just rolls over you. I have never heard anyone else laugh like that. I think it's a super power. Trust me in the magick world and the stuff you must deal with, a good laugh is way better than any potion I could whip up.

"What the hell is so funny? Anyone want to clue me in?" Jay says into the phone with hurt feelings and that just makes it worse. I can picture him at his desk pouting, tapping his pen. Of course, at this time Christine just lets it all out.

"Ok, ok sorry Jay. No nothing is funny. It's just Christine being her normal annoying self", and I pick up a pot holder and throw it at her. Christine turns her head and dunks and it lands on the floor behind her.

"Whatever, sometimes I wonder why we are even friends." He says and hangs up the phone but not before I hear a hint of laughter in his voice.

"Yeah love you too. Christine, you so pissed him off." I laugh because the whole thing was just a little bit funny.

"He will get over it. Besides he's not mad, he just likes to come play with us on our jobs. He's not meant to be a water boy." She tells me.

"Yes, I know but you never hear about the water boy getting hurt or arrested. I mean how do I explain to his boss I'm sorry but Jay stepped into the line of fire and he went boom bursting into pretty blue flames. Yeah I can see that going over really well." I say to her as I head down the hall to take a shower. Christine is just laughing her butt off. I'm so glad she has a sense of humor.

"You might want to turn the water to hot that smell will take forever to come off you. If I were you I would just burn those clothes you have on." Christine says changing the subject as she yells down the hall.

"Gee thanks, Boy love is just pouring in from all kinds of directions. Just so you know I had already planned on burning them. I swear I can feel things crawling on my skin." I yell back.

I shake my hands and arms trying to get the icky off me. There isn't anything on me that you can see with the naked eye but I know there is some nasty bacteria that crawl in the alley ways. I really need to carry hand sanitizer with me on these jobs.

"You know you can probably catch hepatitis C just by being there." She yells again.

"Oh, gee Christine I feel so much better." I slam the bathroom door. I turn on the shower and I can hear her laughing still. *What a butthead!*

CHAPTER 3

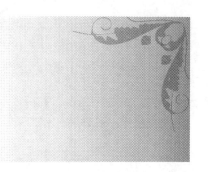

I JUST GOT SETTLED INTO BED with covers pulled to my chin and the phone rings. I look at the clock and it reads midnight. There is only one person who would ever dream of calling me at this hour without thinking of the consequences.

"Someone better be dead or I will see to it", I say answering the phone.

I hear Jay laughing on the other end, "Hey Elements, I need you to meet me at a crime scene."

"Are you freakin kidding me Jay? I just got to bed and I'm exhausted."

"You know I wouldn't ask it of you unless it was serious. I am looking at a dead woman who died brutally and I really could use your insight." You can hear the change in his voice from amusing to serious cop voice.

"What is it?" I ask as I get out of bed already putting my shoes on. I don't need to get dressed because it was chilly tonight so I had sweat pants and a shirt on.

"I really can't go into details over the phone." This usually means he's not standing alone. The other person was probably higher ranked.

"Ok, what's the address?" I ask him as I jot it down on a notepad on the nightstand. "I'm on my way, and Jay?"

"Yeah?" he questions.

"You so owe me for this." I hang up the phone and grab my keys.

A half hour goes by and I arrive at the address but I saw the flashing lights of the cop cars before I even turned onto the street. I park my car and get out as I start combing the area for Jay. The whole time I'm thinking *this so better be worth my losing beauty sleep.*

From behind I hear my name being called out. I was so intent on my search that I walked right passed him. I turn around and see Jay on the phone and I walk up to him during the tail end of his conversation. He is holding his phone between his head and shoulder as he tries to write something down.

"Yes Sir, that's all the information I have right now. I will turn in a full report as soon as I finish up here and the C.S.I team gets done." He hangs up with boss man.

"Thanks Elements for coming out."

"All right lead the way, oh mighty one." I wait until he passes me so I can follow behind him.

About twenty feet ahead of us I could barely make out the outline of a body. I can tell it is a woman though with dark hair like mine. The moon was covered by some clouds but there was enough light to distinguish that.

We arrive at the body and I look down and can see a lot of blood pooling around her frame. I also noticed an object protruding from her chest. I look back over my shoulder, "It looks like a typical stab victim. Why did you need my help for that?" I ask looking at Jay.

"Elements please, I know what it looks like what I want to know is if there is anything unusual about her?"

I turn back to the body and start scanning every detail about her. How it was positioned, if there were any unusual marks that may need a closer look. I squat down close to her face and see that her eyes are half open. I touch her body and she feels warm, "First off, she hasn't been dead for long a couple of hour's tops."

I continue to scan her body and stop at the knife in her chest. My eyes go wide with shock just as the moon shows itself from behind the clouds. I start looking even closer because I so don't feel good about this. Not even a little bit. I take in every detail my dark eyes land on. The way she was dressed, if there was any bruising that could explain anything but I didn't see anything that would help. Well except the knife. She did have a tattoo band around her upper right arm as well as a tattoo of a goddess symbol on her left ankle.

I stand back up and look at Jay, "Have the crews took all the samples they need?"

"Yes, why?" Jay asks because he knows I may be onto something.

"I need you to help me turn the body to its side so I can see if she has any other marks."

Jay pulled out two pairs of rubber gloves handing one to me and he puts the other pair on. Together we turn her over and her shirt rises a little bit. From the flashlight hanging from Jay's mouth I can see some black ink on her lower back. Another tattoo. I lift her shirt and see the whole tat. It was a pentagram with the elements symbols and some hieroglyphics symbols. One I knew because I'm a Virgo too. I roll her back over and take the gloves off.

"Well she was a Virgo", I say getting back up and handing the gloves to Jay so he can throw them away in the hazard bags that are set up at every crime scene. It's where the techs and other cops discard their gloves and the little booties they wear to not get confused with any evidence left by the perp.

"What are you talking about Elements?" Jay asks confused.

"Well right off the bat I can tell you that she was a witch. The pentagram on her back is our sign of protection as well as it symbolizes the four elements. That little M looking thing is the symbol of Virgo."

Jay just stares at me and nods his head. "Is there anything else?" He asks as he looks at the victim.

"Well if I had to guess I would say it is a ritual killing."

Jay snaps his head up and looks at me, "A what?" I can tell I just confused the hell out of him. Just wait until I get to the fun part about the knife.

He goes a little pale which is hard seeing as he has a year-round tan. His skin is the color of chocolate milk.

"A ritual killing. That knife in her chest is no ordinary knife. It is an athame."

"What the hell is an atha… whatever you called it?" He asks me.

"It is a ritual knife witch's use when they are casting a circle. Or as some call it a witch blade."

"Are you telling me this is a supernatural murder?" He says with a little squeak in his voice.

"No, not necessarily", I take a breath to continue. To come up with a better explanation in human terms.

"No what I'm saying is just what I know. For all I know you could be dealing with some sick psychotic who thinks he's the devil reborn. There's supernatural and then there are those who think they are supernatural." Jay just nods his head not knowing how to respond to that.

He starts to rub his head which indicates too much information too fast for him to grasp. You see Jay is new to the magick world. In fact, just since he's known me. I introduced him to it. *Yay me!*

"Well did I help you any?" I ask looking at him.

"You helped a lot. Thank you for coming out here." He walks over to me for a quick hug.

"Anytime, but not at midnight ok?" I give him a return hug and smile.

"Dually noted Elements." He returns my smile.

I start walking back to my car with everything I saw replaying in my mind. "My dear friend you have got your hands full with this one." I say out loud. I look up to the sky and pray for him. Something tells me this is going to get bad and fast. For the first time, I am scared for him.

I also say a prayer for the victim. I know she was a white witch so the magickal world has lost a fallen sister.

I get in my car and start it up to head back home. Maybe I can pick up where I left off and that is a peaceful sleep, but deep down I knew that would not happen. I was arguing with myself for not telling Jay everything. I usually don't leave out information because I do trust him with my life. There was another mark or symbol I didn't tell him about. A mark I am very familiar with because… I have the same one.

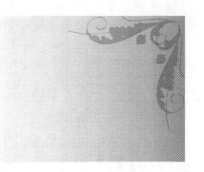

CHAPTER 4

M Y ALARM GOES OFF AND I drag my ass out of bed. Believe me this is no easy task because I am so not a morning person. Sleep eluded me last night when I got back from the crime scene. My mind kept telling me or should I say screaming at me, *you should have told him everything Elements*. Every time I closed my eyes visions of the victim would swim to the surface. It's not like I lied to him, I just didn't tell him everything. So freakin sue me ok! I stumble to the kitchen to start my coffee pot. I can't really think until I have had at least two cups of coffee.

I pick up my kitchen phone and dial Jay's number. He is probably sleeping I smile and think to myself *pay back*.

"Hello", a very tired voice on the other end answers.

"Good morning Jay", and I laugh a little because I can picture a pissed off look on his face.

"You couldn't have waited one more hour?" I hear his bed squeak which means he's probably getting into a sitting position as he rubs his head.

"Why would I do that? I'm trying to catch you off guard, so in a sense I'm helping with your training."

"Ok elements you win. What can I do for you on this fine morning?" I can hear him moving around.

"I was wondering if you could hold off the autopsy of the woman." I ask him sweetly.

"And why would I do that?" and Jay lets out a yawn.

"I want to bring Christine by and see if she can get any hits off her that way we can know where to start the investigation."

"What do you mean by *we*, and how can she help?" He asks questionably.

"Well for starters she will be able to let you know if you are looking for a whack job or a magickal being." I tell him like it's no big deal. You know the whole bringing in civilians on an investigation.

"She's not going to wave her hands above the body and start chanting anything, now is she?" He says with a little humor in his voice.

"Jay, you really are a jerk sometimes you know that?" I can't help but smile because I can picture Christine doing that.

"Ok I can hold it off for twenty-four hours but that is it. My boss is really riding the crew on this one. He doesn't want the town to become scared or think they aren't safe in their own community." He states matter of fact no bull shit. This case is really stirring up questions.

"Ok twenty-four hours. That will be enough. Have a great morning." I hang up smiling and I go get my coffee mug and walk over to the coffee pot.

The mug was a gift from Christine for my birthday. It's purple with red wicked letters that said Witch's Brew. I sit down at the table and open the newspaper. Christine should be calling soon to see if we have anything on the books.

I fold the paper up nothing exciting or new. I start to worry a little because I haven't heard from her yet. Its eight thirty and she hasn't called. I pick up the phone again this time to dial Christine's number. It rings straight to voicemail.

"Shit." I hang up and head to my room to put my clothes on.

"I swear girl if you overslept I am so going to whoop your ass." I say out loud to my empty house.

Although I say this just to feel better and calm myself but something is not right. My *Oh shit detector* is binging like crazy. I head to my car and dial her number again with my cell phone and it still rings to voicemail. I hit the button on my key chain and my trunk pops up. I start looking over my supplies to make sure I have everything I will need in case this turns into a metaphysical battle and we might need some magick to get our asses out of it.

I unzip my bag and take stock of everything.

Potions... Check.

Candles... Check.

Salt... Check.

When all else fails, I have my Glock lock and loaded. I can already feel my adrenaline pumping through my veins. I close the trunk and get in my car and throw the gear shift into drive. I peel out of my driveway with my tires squealing. That should make for a nice wake up call for my neighbors. *Who needs a rooster! Good morning.*

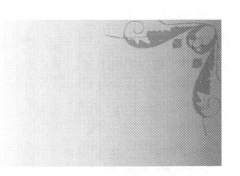

CHAPTER 5

I MAKE IT TO CHRISTINE'S HOUSE in record time. Hawthorne is usually about a thirty-minute drive and I get there in fifteen. Thank goodness, I didn't see any cops or deputies on the road. I would have so gotten like three tickets, going over the speed limit, not using my blinker when switching lanes, and running a red light and that's just what I could come up with. Who knows what they would have come up with?

I parked my car under a big oak tree she has in her front yard. I jump out of my car running to her front door yelling, "Christine?"

I reach for the door handle just as some force field activates. It throws me through the air, "Mother Fu…" I hit the ground hard landing on my ass about ten feet from the door. At least my detector wasn't lying. There was something major and magickal too going down here.

I get back on my feet dusting the dirt and gravel off my butt and hands and start walking backwards to my car. I should have grabbed some potions before I took off. *What a dumbass move Elements.*

I reach my trunk and send my psychic tentacles out scanning the area as my eyes do the same thing. They say your eyes can pick up movement before your mind can register it. I grab a couple of my potions and start walking towards her house again. "Christine, Are you alright?"

My eyes land on a quartz crystal that is at the foot of her door, *good girl, you do listen to me.* I know they go all the way around her house. I look at it again and notice that it is dark in color glowing black, "Shit that's not a good sign."

It means something is here playing with the dark forces. Dark magick. I take a relaxing breath and open my third eye and mind so that I can pick up on it. A tingly sensation comes back to me. "Bingo… All right asshole I know you're here!" I yell out as my eyes start scanning for every single hiding spot. Which is a lot because Christine has so many trees on her property that any of them can be a hiding place.

She has Maple trees, Oak trees, Weeping Willows, and who knows what else. I swear it looks like she has a tree farm. It's a wonder how they even got a house in here. She also has a couple fairy gardens which are quite beautiful when you get to see the flowers in bloom. Fairies are great at keeping flowers and plants alive and vibrant. They are what we call Elementals and are very protective of the Earth and all her greenery.

"Come on… I am really not in the mood to play hide-n-seek!" I look around very slowly as I put my shield up.

"Why don't you show yourself and we can play a real game of survival of the fittest!" I pin point the location to a huge Oak tree in her back yard.

I can hear Christine yelling at me from inside her house. "Elements I can't open my door!"

"It's ok Christine." I yell back over my shoulder. There is no way I'm taking my eyes off that tree. That's all the enemy needs. That one weakness, the one look away and then they get you.

"Can you use your phone?" I ask her waiting for her response. I get hit with the first psychic hit and it knocks me to the ground.

I'm lucky my shield took the brunt of the force. I still went down and yes it hurts. When you get hit it feels like an air pressure force against you as if you were standing in front of an airplane as it starts its engine or like a wind stream only you can feel.

"No, just some flippin static!" By now I can hear the fear in her voice. She is scared.

I know she's got to be hurting as well. You can't be this close to evil magick and not feel pain when you are a sensitive. If this doesn't get handled quickly she will become sick and be out of commission for at least twenty-four hours.

"Shit! Ok Christine hold on!" I push my button on my ear piece, "Call DJ". It plays back in my ear calling Detective Jay.

It rings three times and he finally picks up, "Talk to me." I can hear him shuffling some papers. Good he's already at the office.

"Jay!" I say out of breath and with clenched teeth. I'm trying to talk to Jay at the same time maintain my hold on my shield. *Not so easy!*

"What's wrong Elements?" He asks with a panic filled voice.

"I'm calling in my favor… Now!" I get to my feet again a little steadier and gaining control. I have a few little cuts and scratches on my palms when I tried to break my fall but they were already healing and closing. *Can I get a Yee-haw for magick?*

"What do you need me to do?" He asks ready to do my bidding. I can hear him getting out of his chair at work.

"I need you to head over to Christine's house A.S.A.P. and don't do the speed limit!" I hang up on him and in total control again. I get into fighting stance sending a hit out to whoever.

"That was a cheap shot. I thought all you bad asses were tough?"!

That comment must have egged him on because at that moment someone steps from behind the tree. I have my gun aimed at the tree with one hand and with the other I have a potion in it.

I can see a young boy maybe twenty years old if that with a little peach fuzz on his chin. "Are you serious? I mean really are you freaking kidding me?" I'm taken off guard a bit by his looks.

"What are you, ten, twelve at the most?" I bring my arm down which turn out to be a not so smart move.

He sees this mistake and throws a hit at me but I see it in time to put my shield up. The hit reverberates off me and bounces back towards him which causes him to fall against the tree.

I hear a car pull up behind me and pray that it is Jay. The kid sends another hit causing me to smack the ground knocking the wind out of me. I try and catch my breath without it hurting and get back up but slowly.

"Elements!" Jay yells running towards me.

"No!" I throw my arm back in a stay back position. "I'm ok. Go help Christine. She is trapped in her house because her doors will not open!" Jay turns around and starts running back to the front of the house.

Jay is at the front door trying to shove it open with his shoulder and bangs on the door. "Christine… It's me".

"Oh Jay!" He can hear the excitement in her voice. "I can't open the door. The damn crystals won't let me!"

"What?" he says confused.

"The crystals. The white rocks by the door. They have to be moved. Well actually only one of them has to be moved and then the circle will be broken." She says from the other side of the door praying he will understand but knowing he won't.

"What… There's no circle." He looks for anything that resembles a circle on the ground.

Christine is on the other side of the door shaking her head, "It figures he would only hear part of it." She mumbles to herself.

"Ok Jay listen carefully. The crystals are protecting me and my house. You can't see the circle because it's magick so stop looking around." He looks up to see if she is watching him from a window because that's exactly what he was doing.

"What the hell are you talking about? What circle? What magick?" He says all confused.

"Listen Jay all you have to do is kick one of the crystals away and the circle will be broken. Do you understand that?"

"Yeah", and he pulls back his foot and does just that. He kicks the crystal like a soccer ball. It goes flying through the air. Jay turns around when he hears the click of the door opening.

Christine comes out and joins Jay on the porch just in time to see the crystal land about six feet away. "You know a simple nudge would have worked." She says to him and laughs.

Jay shoots her a go to hell look and flips her the bird. She stifles the laugh with a cough. Jay sees the laughter in her eyes and gives in and starts laughing himself.

"You know I'm still new to this stuff." He waves his hand around him meaning magick, crystals, and circles you can't see.

Christine and Jay head towards the back yard to try and help Elements. Just as they turn the corner Christine stumbles and dizziness consumes her. "Whoa!" Jay sees this and grabs her elbow.

"What's wrong?" He grabs his gun out of reflex and starts looking around.

"There is some major mojo going on back here!" Christine shakes her head clear. Jay returns his gun to its holster.

He just grabbed it out on instinct because in his line of work all it takes is a few seconds to get killed.

They start running to my side just as I get up from the ground and throw something towards the tree.

"Plug your ears!" I yell just as a loud explosion rings out and something by the tree erupts into blue flames and then poof it disappears.

"What the hell…" Jay uncovers his ears, "was that?" He looks at me.

"That my friend was a BBU going bye bye." I walk over to Christine and give her a hug.

"Are you alright?" I pull back and look at her. To see if there were any side effects from her being this close to magick. *You use magick, magick will use you back*

"Hey, what about me? I kicked the crystal out of the way." I laugh and go give him a hug too.

"You're right Jay, Thanks for saving our asses!" We all bust out laughing because sometimes that's all you can do especially in our line of work. If you don't your mind can start playing tricks on you.

This could have turned ugly I mean really ugly. If you sit and think about it, well it can freeze you when you can't afford to be frozen. It's them or us, and I always bet on us.

The three of us turn and go back to the front yard so I can shut my door, seeing as I didn't have time when I got here. Jay and I enter Christine's house. "What's for breakfast?" Jay asks.

I shake my head. He is hopeless. I look over my shoulder and see Christine bend over and pick up her crystal and walks back to her door and puts it back in its place. The circle reactivates and she shuts her door.

CHAPTER 6

WE ARRIVE AT THE MORGUE because I want Christine to see if she can read anything off the body. It is not one of her favorite things to do because she doesn't like working off dead people. After I explained why we needed her to do it she was all in. Anything to help that's my Christine.

Jay and I are standing to the side to give her space. It's always an amazing experience to watch her do her thing. If it were any other person looking on it would look like some woman just walking around and starring down at a body. If you have magickal eyes you would see her whole body has a glowing white circle around it. When the colors change that's some form of information she has collected. She could almost tell you the whole life story of the person.

We don't interrupt her or ask questions until it's over. Jay and I just stand there in silence. When she pulls her glow in then she will tell us everything we need to know.

Jay is leaning against the wall while Christine is in her element so to speak. He whispers to me, "Elements", as he asks me to come her with his finger.

"What?" I whisper back harshly and lean my five foot seven frame against the wall on his right side. I feel very short next to him because he is a little over six feet tall.

I hate even whispering, because it's quite amazing to watch Christine when she's at work. It's like your very own window into the northern lights. There are different colors flying around and she in a trance like state. She doesn't even feel us here right now. It takes every ounce of her concentration to obtain information this way.

"All it looks like she is doing is standing there starring at the body." Jay whispers and looks back at her trying to see anything that seems weird or magickal.

"Shhh, let her finish" and that was the end of this conversation.

There was no talking until she was done. Jay crosses his arms and does a little huff. I just smile because sometimes he is so a kid. She pulls her glow in and looks over at me. The look on her face tells me this is so not going to be good. Jay pulls from the wall first and walks towards her looking her up and down. He just walks in a slow deliberate circle around her. He is trying to see if something magickal just happened.

"What are you doing Jay?" Christine asks putting her hands on her hips.

"I'm just trying to see whatever she sees", as he points his head in my direction.

"I can fix that for you. All it takes is a little potion and poof you will be able to see magick." I tell him knowing he is against altering himself in anyway magickal or otherwise.

"Not funny!" He says as he turns and walks out of the room a head of us.

Christine and I stifle our laugh because he looks back at us with the, *no freakin way so don't even think about it* look. We stare at the ground and start following behind him as if we were children who just got scolded for missing curfew.

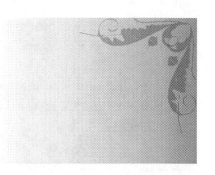

CHAPTER 7

W E ARE BACK AT MY house and Christine heads straight for the coffee pot and starts making some. I know with one look at her she will know what I kept from Jay. *Boy is this going to be fun!* I mean not that I am making a joke out of this because this is so not the time to try my hand in comedy but sarcastically this is going to be fun.

I look over at Jay who is sitting at the kitchen table trying to be patient and wait for Christine to start explaining what she saw. He's losing the battle because he starts tapping his hands on the dark wood table, tap, tap like he's playing the drums.

Christine sits down at the head of the table and gives me a stern look. "First off your victim and that little incident at my house this morning is related." She says looking at Jay who has stopped playing the drums and stares at Christine.

"The same dark energy I felt this morning is the same as the energy I got off your victim." I just plop my head down onto the table and look sideways at her.

"Are you sure?" Christine gives me the look, *yes, I'm sure.*

"It is a message for someone her at the table." She looks straight at me.

I take a deep breath and let it out slowly, "Ok I knew it was for me as soon as I saw the athame sticking out of the victim's chest." I am really pissed off right now. I mean you have something to say to me, send me an email or text message. Don't go out and kill someone. *Asshole.*

Jay gives me a stern look. I know he's mad at me but oh well he'll get over it. I can already tell it won't be the last time he gets pissed at me either. I just didn't know how to tell them. It's not something you talk about since most times Covens prefer silence and secrecy.

"Ok a few years back I was part of a coven but due to my powers I was asked to leave because they thought I wouldn't be able to control them. There is a symbol on the hilt of the athame that I have as well." I stand up and turn around lifting my long dark brown hair off my neck so I can show them. It was two B's facing each other which symbolized Blessed Be on the nape of my neck.

I turn back around and let go of my hair as it fall back in place and then I sit down again. Jay is looking at me like I lied to him which I didn't. I just neglected to say anything and to him it is the same as lying. He will forgive me, it's just that he will give me hell until he does.

Christine takes a deep breath and holds it in for a few seconds before releasing. "That's not all I saw." She closes her eyes to recount everything.

"It's not over. This is only the beginning. He and I say he because that's the sense of energy I felt. He's not done. He already has his next victim picked and tonight she will die."

This makes sense to me because it is the cycle of the full moon. Tonight, is her first night and any super natural being, the good, the bad, and the ugly will all have extra strength with their given powers.

You gotta love the full moon. Since the full moon has three nights we have two nights left to catch the creep. If he is this powerful now, then we too will need the strength of the full moon behind us. This is so going to be messy. I look over at Christine and I can see tears in her eyes that she is holding back. *Uh oh, this can't be good.*

"There's something else you're not saying isn't there Christine?" I reach out and take her hand.

Christine squeezes my hand tightly as if to make sure I'm real. She nods her head yes, "I saw you dead with a knife sticking out of your chest."

I take a deep breath and let it out so quietly that you couldn't even hear me exhale. The whole time I was listening to Christine I was thinking of a plan that leaves us among the living.

"That's not going to happen Christine. We will change that so don't even waste your time thinking of it ok?" I tell her with more confidence than I felt.

I am trying to put both at ease. I don't want them worrying about me. I don't think it worked but a girl must try. They both are looking at me with these sober expressions on their face.

Christine shakes herself clear before she continues. "It felt like this person wanted to leave that impression because he knew you would be involved in this case. You know him Elements, and he knows you." She takes a mini break then continues. "I also kept picking up and this is going to sound crazy but I kept picking up the smell of outdoors and cats. Does that make sense to you?" She looks over at me.

My eyes open wide and I damn near choke on a breath. I know exactly who she's talking about. Now this case just went to all kinds of shit in a matter of minutes. *There is no way he's back I kept telling myself over and over. It can't be him. Before my mind would wrap around that idea I knew it to be false. There was only one cat I know and yes, we did have a common enemy.*

"Phenix." I say a bare whisper slipping from my mouth. I put my hands under my head for cushion because I was about to star banging it against the table. I so don't need a headache right now.

"Who?" They both ask in union and look at me for an explanation.

I put my head down and calm myself with cleansing breaths that are so not working. I knew this day would come. I just wasn't expecting it to come with a bang. Then again Phenix never does anything he doesn't put his whole heart into. I know from personal experience about the way he does things. At least that's how he was when we were together. *Phenix.*

CHAPTER 8

P HENIX AND I WERE TOGETHER for a long time. I knew he was a shape shifter before I even knew his name. He is a panther. Actually, if you looked at him it wasn't a stretch of the imagination to see it. Even in human form he had panther like qualities. He was very well toned and he has a grace about him that reminds you of a cat. He even had the coloring in human form.

He has black hair that he kept very well trimmed. His eyes were so dark you could drown in them. His skin was a golden tan all year round like the Native Americans. In fact, the panther was his family's tribal animal. His voice whenever he spoke sent ripples down your spine. It was almost like a purr a cat does.

It wasn't just me either, other women noticed him and felt it too. You could see it in their eyes staring off in a dream like state as if he was the best thing in the whole world. Now imagine trying to go shopping with him. They would literally stop what they were doing just to watch him.

It's the whole grace thing that makes you feel lucky just being next to him. I guess you could say I fell hard and fast. I still have very strong feelings for him even though it's been a couple of years since I had last seen him. I can't believe for one minute that he is behind this thing. My gut tells me there is something more and someone else and I always go with my gut. In the deepest part of my mind I know he is being set up. All I have to do is figure out who it is, kill them and then find Phenix and whoop his ass for leaving without a goodbye or anything. See nice and easy.

"Who is Phenix, Elements?" Christine turns to me with her hazel eyes waiting for an answer.

I just stare at her. I shake myself to come back to the kitchen. My mind left there for a minute.

"It's someone from my past and I know he has no part in this. He would never do this to anyone especially a witch and a white witch at that." I say with anger and look at them with my guard up. I know it's not her fault after all she is just telling us what she pulled from the victim.

"Whoa girl, back up and check yourself. Don't shoot the messenger." Christine tells me. I can also see in her eyes that she isn't blaming him. She was just doing the job that was asked of her.

"You're right Christine. I'm sorry, but I'm very protective when it comes to Phenix." I exhaled and laid my head on the table for the umpteenth time. If I keep doing this, I'm going to have a permanent imprint of my fingers on my fore head.

Christine looks at me and takes my hand in hers like a mother would do and tries to console me. She starts drawing little relaxing circles on the back of my palm to sooth me.

"I don't know who this Phenix is, so I will not assume it's him doing this, but Elements how can you be so sure he isn't involved?"

I look at her with tears in my eyes, "Because we were a couple and I know he loved me." A tear slips down my cheek leaving a tiny wet trail.

Jay uses this time to interrupt by clearing his throat. He always gets uncomfortable when emotions start flying especially women who are emotional. What is it with guys and girls crying?

"Well Elements", he looks a way so I can wipe my tears from my face. "Do you have any idea who would do something like this?"

"Well I can think of a lot of people, how about most of the dark world for starters. Or someone who has been trained in the dark forces of magick? We can't even exclude humans. There are so many books out there that have surfaced on magick. It only takes someone who is patient enough to read and understand the contents that they could pull it off." I say to Jay who is still very new to the magick world himself. This may just be too much for him to comprehend.

Yes, I know he hangs out with a witch and a sensitive fighting crime together but so what right? He is still very human and a man on top of that, so there's a lot of repeating stuff.

Christine gets up and pours some more coffee, this is her crutch. Her security blanket so to speak. Whenever she is nervous or worried out comes the coffee and the coffee pot. Needless to say, I buy in bulk.

"Ok. Let's clear our heads and figure this shit out." Did I mention she cusses too when she is scared?

I find it hard to believe sometimes because she is so mellow that any cuss word even damn sounds weird in her southern accent.

"We are not stupid here. We have a little information to get us started so we are not going in blind. I mean of course I would love more information like their plan step by step but hey let's work with what we have." She returns to her chair at the table spilling some coffee because she put her mug down a little too hard and it sloshed over the edge. That's my girl straight to business.

"Listen girl, we will solve this and we will all be sitting at this very table when it's all said and done doctoring our wounds, so calm down and put that powerful mind of yours to work." I give her a smile and a wink.

"Jay, can you go back through the case file again and see if we are missing anything, even if you feel that it is so mundane that it's not worth mentioning. The more info we have the better prepared we can be for whoever this asshole is that is messing up our world."

He laughs at me and shakes his head, "Remind me to never piss you off. I so don't want to be on the receiving end of that temper or the little pink bottle that goes Boom."

I get up from the table and start to walk to my room. I can hear them pushing their chairs out so they can follow.

"What are you going to do?" They ask on top of pushing their chairs back in.

"I am going to dip into my witch's box and find my list of contacts."

"Contacts for what?" with questioning eyes.

I can just picture the looks on their faces and it puts a smile on mine.

"Just put it this way, the names on the list aren't friends but allies. They owe me a favor or two. Everyone I have ever helped in the super natural world is on there and I believe it's time for me to call in my favors."

There is no way they are going to miss getting a peek of the mystical witch box. I haven't told them that it's just a storage box for candles, potions, and other supplies you need for magickal purposes. I wouldn't want to take the mystery out of it for them. After all what kind of witch would I be if I ruin that for them? Not a very good one.

I just look back over my shoulder and shake my head laughing to myself. This is going to be fun. Can I get a Yee-Haw! I open the box and a smell of frankincense swarms your nostrils. Yes, I know not the best smelling incense but a very powerful one. It wards off negativity.

I pull out some of the stuff in it and find my black velvet bag that held the list for protection so it wouldn't get ruined. I glance at the list scanning names and my eyes settle on one name. This person is not friend but she is a bad ass and someone you want on your side if ever in a fight. *Sirus... no last name but I do have a number to reach her at or leave a message for her.*

I grab my phone and dial it..." Hey this message is for Sirus just tell her it's her favorite witch". The beep ended and I hang up.

She will get back to me; the only problem is the waiting game. In other words, she will return the call but not before she is ready too. Like I said before she is a bad ass but she is worth the wait. I'm very confident that she'll show up because the girl can't turn down a fight no matter who or what she is up against.

CHAPTER 9

J AY WAS FORCED AWAKE FROM sleep because he heard noises right outside his bedroom window. He has always been a light sleeper it's kind of a requirement when you become a detective. You never know when your phone is going to ring and you have to head out to a crime scene.

He grabs his gun from under his pillow and proceeds out of his bedroom to the stairs. His eyes search the darkness for anything that moves and brings his gun up to chest level in case he must shoot. If you hold your gun up this high, no matter how tall you are you will manage to hit your target.

He reaches the landing which is half way between up and down stairs he does a quick left, right turn of his head. He jumps when he sees his own reflection in the mirror. The episode at Christine's house and everything they have been through thus far has put him on high alert and made him high strung. He shakes his head and makes a mental note to take the damn mirror down in the morning.

Jay continues down the rest of the stairs and walks over to the living room window. He opens the curtains just a little so he can peer out. He sees nothing out of the ordinary just an empty street and the full moon and puts the curtains back in place. He walks over to the front door and unlocks it so he can step out to the porch. He does another quick left, right head turn seeing nothing out there.

He scratches his head, "Maybe I just imagined the noise after all this case is making me nervous."

He puts his gun down at his side and shakes everything off. "Ok Jay, you seriously need a vacation, and maybe some new friends."

When he turns to go back in he feels something brush his leg and hears, "Meow."

He looks down and sees a beautiful white cat rubbing against him. "Aren't you a pretty thing?" He reaches down and picks the cat up to take it into to the house with him. The cat automatically starts purring and Jay smiles.

He places the cat on the floor as he locks the front door again. He walks towards the kitchen and starts talking to the cat over his shoulder, "Well girl, I don't have any food for you but I will pour you some milk." The cat starts following at his heels.

Jay puts a bowl of milk down, "In the morning we will figure out what to do with you."

Jay turns the light on above the stove for the cat and turns the rest of the lights off. "Good night."

Jay walks out of the kitchen and heads towards the stairs. He softly whistles to himself as he walks up the stairs to go back to bed. He really has had too much excitement in just a short while. This case is going to open his eyes to a whole new world literally. He just hopes he's got what it takes to survive and understand all this crap.

The cat looks up at the ceiling as if it can see through it to the room above. Its ears perk up listening to anything that makes noise. It hears Jay shut his bedroom door and turn off the light getting into bed with a squeak of the bed frame.

Down stairs in the kitchen a gentle breeze starts to stir and a little wind tornado appears. The cat has vanished and in its place stood a pale blond hair woman with green eyes. She heads for the stairs and starts walking up them never making a sound. Cats are quiet like that.

CHAPTER 10

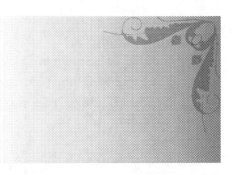

I WAKE UP FROM A RESTLESS sleep because my instincts tell me something is not quite right. You know the feeling you get in the pit of your stomach before something bad happens? Well it's like that. I reach over and turn on my bedside lamp. I pick up the phone and dial a number. While I am waiting for and answer a very sleepy voice comes on.

"HELLO?" AND YOU HEAR THEM yawn.

"Hey Christine, it's me."

Hey Elements, is everything alright?"

"I don't know. I just have a weird vibe going on so I figured I'd call you. Are you ok?"

"Yeah, I just went to bed about an hour ago. I'm trying to fight off a migraine." She tells me

"I am sorry about the headache. I will let you go so you can sleep. I'm going to check in with Jay."

We hang up and I say a little healing spell for Christine and send it via the cosmic phone lines. I start dialing Jay's number. While I'm waiting for him to answer my gut instincts go into hyper drive. *Oh shit, come on Jay. Hurry up and answer.*

"Detective Stone," a voice full of alert answers.

"Hey Jay, its Elements."

"What is it Elements, I just got back into bed." I hear him yawn trying to stay awake.

"Yeah sorry about the time, but I just wanted to see if everything is alright? My stomach is doing flip flops."

"Everything is fine. There was a little excitement but it's good now." Jay says through another yawn.

"What kind of excitement?" I am so uptight I feel I'm ready to pop. I hate feeling like this.

If I could just find other magickal friends, I wouldn't have to worry so much and feel like I must be a super hero.

"It was nothing just some noise outside and upon investigating it turned out to be a cat."

"What?"

"A cat, and its actually quite pretty …"

"Jay" I say interrupting him, "How long have you lived there in that house?"

"Five or six years…Why?" His voice changes to alertness.

"In all that time, how many times have you ever seen a cat and a stray one at that?"

"Well this is the first," just as he finished I hear his bedroom door crash into the wall.

"Shit! Who the hell are you? "Jay yells and the phone falls to the floor.

"Jay, Jay what the hell is going on?" I scream into the phone as I walk to the closet to get my shoes.

I can hear Jay talking to me but it sounds distant and muffled because the phone is on the floor.

"Elements! There some woman in my room and something freaky going on with her eyes!"

I calm down a bit because I know exactly who it is but I am totally pissed at her and I will take care of it. She is scaring the shit out of my friend playing her damn jokes on mortals. She really is a bitch I was not exaggerating.

"Jay, first calm down, but don't look into her eyes." I hear him pick up the phone.

"What… This is your back up? Sirus?"

"Tell Sirus to cut her shit and get her ass over to my house." He looks over at the woman who is laughing.

"Oh, big bad detective scared of a little pussy… cat?" Sarcasm just dripping with every word from Sirus. She breaks into more laughing.

"How the hell did you get into my house?" He asks her.

"Why Jay, you brought me in." She says.

Jay looks confused now. "Let me guess our little witch didn't tell you what I am did she?"

Jay returns his attention back to me on the phone. "Umm Elements is there something you forgot to tell me? "I hear his voice change from scared to annoyance. If I didn't know any better I would say pissed. He sounds very pissed.

His voice totally changes. I wonder if it's the voice he uses when he is interrogating perps. A small shiver runs down my spine. I have never met that side of him before and I'm kind of thinking I don't want too.

"Well shit, and damn. I'm sorry Jay. I thought I would have more time. She usually keeps me waiting so long that if it were possible I would die of old age.

I am so racking up the points. First I keep some information from him about the case and second I didn't tell him about Sirus. I'm going for major cool friend award here.

"Elements…I'm waiting." Jay says through tight lips trying to hold his tongue and not cuss my ass out.

"Ok, Sirus is a shape shifter. She can change into any cat form from domestic house cat to the cheetah or any in between there."

Sirus can hear my side of the conversation due to a cat's great hearing and she laughs. "Gee everyone's favorite little witch kept another secret."

What a bitch. Wait until she gets here. I will show her favorite.

"Jay I'm sorry just tell Sirus to leave and get to my house and we will take care of this tomorrow."

I can hear Jay take a deep breath. He really is pissed. I'm beginning to wonder if I have under estimated Jay and his temper. He must have given Sirus one of those looks because all I heard before he hung up on me was, *ok, ok I'm leaving. We are on the same side… this time. I'm leaving the house.*

Yes, he is pissed. He hung up on me without saying anything. I feel an urge to walk over to my window and look out. This full moon is so messing up my world this month. I pull the curtains back and look out into the night. My eyes are drawn to the street light. I look even harder and there is someone standing there. I know exactly who that someone is. "Phenix."

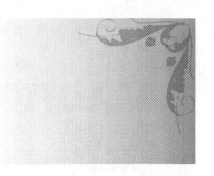

CHAPTER 11

I WALK DOWN THE HALL TO get to the front door and I can't help the way my heart is pounding. Phenix has always done that to me. It's like his whole energy reaches out and caresses me like a lovers' touch. His lips have the same effect. What can I say I'm a slave for him and he knows it? When he left without a trace I went crazy so to speak. I was sad, pissed, and angry. I never got the closure of why he left.

I open the front door and step out onto my porch. *Ok Elements stay calm, and for goddess sake don't swoon. Whatever you do, do not look at his lips or think of his hands. You can so do this girl!*

"What do you want Phenix?" My voice waivers a little but I think I did a good job at covering it up. *Yeah right! He's a freakin cat... Remember.*

"Is that all I get Elements?" He gives me the look that always made me melt. It still has that same effect. Right now, all I want to do is run into his arms.

"That is all you deserve, you're an asshole. You walked out on me without an explanation, a kiss my butt or anything. What do you expect?" I try and calm myself down which is hard to do because I do have a strong temper. When it goes, there is no stopping it.

In fact, my temper got me into so much trouble as a child that even now I still have problems curving it.

"Ok, you are right. I deserve that, but I couldn't tell you why and I need you to know that I did what I had too for you." He reaches out to caress my face. While his voice changes sending shivers down my spine. *Don't let him touch you Elements. You will lose and he knows it.*

I step back bringing my hand up which is holding a knife. "Don't even think about it Phenix. Pull your power in." I do this more for me than him. If I were to cut him he would just heal almost immediately.

I just know if he touches me I will lose whatever control I still have. It's not much.

He pulls his hand back and I can see the wounded look in his eyes. I know it hurt him. He hurt me so what goes around comes around.

"Elements I need your help. I can't do this by myself. It's going to take more than just me to get through it. I can admit I don't have the strength to fight him off."

I hold my hand up to silence him. "I know all about it Phenix. You are being framed for murder and I know it's more than one. I also have a pretty good idea on the who but I could be wrong on that. After all I have racked up a lot of enemies in the last few years. Where I am stuck is the why?"

"How do you know? You have spies watching me?" He says with a smile on his lips. *As if I don't but he doesn't have to know that.*

"Oh please… Don't flatter yourself. I know because we have already seen the first victim and we have had a little run in so to speak."

I turn away quickly because my eyes were starting to trace the lines of his lips. *You're a stupid little witch. Where is a house falling from the sky when you need one? Why can't you control yourself around him? Your emotions take over and you are useless against his power.*

"Did he hurt you?" I can see him turn angry and worrying about my well-being. *Oh, gee he still cares. But he couldn't say bye, could he? Calm down girl. You are losing control of your temper again.*

"No, it wasn't me. They tried to get rid of a friend of mine." I start to smile because I see jealously cross his eyes instantly.

"This friend, Man or woman?" He asks with a very stubborn stance and a lilt to his voice.

"Oh Phenix, jealousy so not a good look on you." I'm excited because I am enjoying all the different emotions I see his face go through.

I know evil, right? So, sue me ok. He deserves to squirm a little bit, maybe I'll just keep it up. Yeah right. You will falter you always do. They say there is a true love for everyone. I know in my heart he is mine.

"Look I know you are pissed at me but I can't explain why I did it. At least not yet. Will you please trust me?" His eyes show so much, begging please, that I can feel myself faltering.

"Whatever, but if you jet out again without a goodbye this time I will hunt you down, then kill you, then raise you back from the dead just to kill you again, understand?" I am trying so hard not to smile because I can see his cheek twitching trying not to laugh. He always said he loved it when I got angry because my eyes turn to brown fire whatever the hell that means.

"You're the boss", and he laughs.

He looks into my eyes and moves forward slowly. *Don't fall for him again girl.* I feel his lips touch mine in a sensual kiss. I close my eyes and lean into him and our kiss deepens and fill with passion. His hands start roaming over my body and I do the same to him. I feel his muscles tense under my touch as they linger on his chest and then I move around to his back. I always did love his chest. His muscles are small but perfect. I never did like big bulky men. It just doesn't look good to me. It was like he was sculptured by the Greek gods themselves to give the mortals a mouth watery reaction. He was gorgeous.

I pull back out of breath and put both my hands on his chest to push him back a little. I'm not to convincing because he can see me struggling with my own body's reaction. I know exactly what I want and I know it will happen. I can see he wants the same thing.

My body is already trembling and anticipating his next touch. He can make me wet instantly just by touch. A Greek God.

"Phenix we can't do this now." I tell him as I command my body to behave. Which is so hard to do because it's been a very long time since I have been with a man. In fact, the last time I was, was with him.

"Elements I never stopped caring and I can't help the way my body reacts when I'm in your presence." He says pulling me into him and wrapping his arms around me like a protective wall.

He leans down and gives me another passionate kiss and this time there was no pulling back. I have lost. Now all I can think about is how quick we can get to my room and how fast can our clothes come off.

I can hear my mind laughing at my utter loss of control. He picks me up and carries me into the house and down the hall to the bedroom without missing a step. He does have cat like reflexes. As he lays me gently on the bed he pulls my shirt off at the same time. *Very smooth!*

I help him with the rest of my clothes and his. He moves his body over mine and comes down for a kiss.

Our bodies are moving together as one and reacting the same as always, very wet, very fast. I wasn't the only one who lost this battle. His body was standing at attention from the moment of our second kiss outside. It's nice to know he can't control himself either.

I hear my front door open and Sirus yells out, "Honey I'm home." She heads down the hall to my room. *Shit, too late,* she sticks her head in, "Hey Elements! Whoa my bad." She ducks back out shutting the door.

Phenix looks at me, "Sirus, you called her for Hel", and the door opens again before he could finish his sentence.

Both Phenix and I look at her. Sirus sticks her head in and looks Phenix up and down in a slow caress with her eyes, "Nice!" She shuts the door again and I can hear her laughing as she walks down the hall. She goes to the kitchen and opens the fridge to find something to eat.

"Like I was saying before you asked Sirus for help?" He looks down on me with a smirk.

"Did I ever tell you that you talk way too much?" With that he smiles and leans down for a kiss.

CHAPTER 12

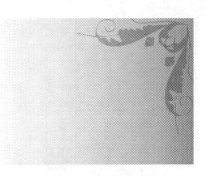

I T'S ABOUT TEN O'CLOCK IN the morning and we are all sitting at the kitchen table discussing the murder, how to clear Phenix's name and figure out who the jackass is that's behind this whole mess. *No big deal. Easy crap. Hell, it could be complicated.*

"OK whoever is behind this wants to take over the underworld, and get rid of us and come out clean smelling like a rose." I said looking at each one of them sitting here at the table.

Phenix reaches under the table and squeezes my thigh for comfort. Mine not his.

I am so scared that I'm going to lose one of them or more before this whole thing is done with. Phenix can see that in my eyes, that is why he touches me for my comfort. After all they say the eyes are the window into the soul. He has always been able to read me like a book, which sucks because I was never able to surprise him because he always figured it out.

I honestly can't see my life without any of them in it. Christine is my best friend in the whole world. Jay is like a brother to me. You know the kind of relationship that can bitch about each other but let someone else do it and you are all over their ass. Phenix I believe is the love of my life, and then there is Sirus. I wouldn't call us friends, in fact in the back of each of our minds we wonder who is the better fighter out of us. If it came to blows who would win? I think we are both too scared to find out the answer to that question so we leave it alone.

I still wouldn't want any harm to come to her. She came to help me out which translates into me taking a bullet for her if it comes down to it.

"Well our bad guy struck again, last night." Jay says bringing us all back to the main discussion.

"What?" Christine asks with a worry filled voice because of the vision she had of me. She really is bothered by it.

I keep telling her that the vision is not going to come true but it doesn't stop her from worrying. She picks up her coffee takes a sip and looks at me just to make sure I'm still here. She is always worrying about me. I keep telling her I can take care of myself but she worries anyways. If she cares for you, she thinks it's her job to protect you. Sometimes I wonder why she hasn't bought me a pair of safety tip scissors yet.

In fact, it would not surprise me if one day she looks at my tennis shoes and say, "Make sure you tie those in double knots." I smile to myself because I can so see her doing that.

"Yeah, the victim, a woman in her twenties, stabbed to death with her athame." Jay looks at me very proud because he remembered what a witch's knife is called.

"We actually got her coven to talk with us and release some information about her. They also invited us to their healing ritual to participate in it. Whatever the hell that is." Jay shrugs his shoulder at me and I roll my eyes at him.

He still has a hard time with magick. Which is ironic considering his best friend is a witch. Not to mention a sensitive as well as a shape shifter. The whole time he is talking he keeps shooting Sirus dirty looks. I would probably react the same way if I went through what he did last night. Sirus just looks at him with all innocent eyes, "What", then she cracks a smile.

Did I tell you that she is a bitch? She is defiantly one you want on your side. She is someone you don't want to cross paths with.

Christine is picking up on the vibes from them because she keeps fidgeting with her hands. "Something I should know about you two?" She looks at Jay and then Sirus. You can see goosebumps breaking out on her skin. Whenever there is magick or the energy shifts around people she gets goosebumps

"No not really, Sirus kind of surprised him last night and he is still pissed." I tell Christine but I can't help but smile. It is funny.

"Surprise how?" she asks looking at Jay for an explanation.

"She tricked me to get in my house. She was a cat I thought she was lost so I brought her in my house and then poof she's a woman and she does some freaky weird thing with her eyes. I swear I almost had a heart attack." Jay tells her with anger dripping off each word. He gives Sirus a *drop-dead look. If looks could kill Sirus would be dead.*

I swear if anyone else over heard this conversation they would think we are all crazy, and right now Jay doesn't sound too far off. I wonder if he even knows how weird he sounds talking like this. Probably not!

Christine looks at me confused. "Sirus is a shape shifter. She can change into any cat form from your little house cat to a tiger or anything that falls in between them." I tell Christine as I kick Sirus in the ankle under the table.

I swear Sirus always has to do something. She can't just come and listen to directions. I know she is biting her tongue right now to keep from laughing. If I were her I would watch it. Jay might just pull his gun out and shoot, and say *oops.* Well then again Sirus wouldn't be Sirus if she followed instructions or paid attention to the hints and looks she gets from people.

Christine is looking at her like some freak on display which I guess I couldn't blame her. I would too, if I were normal, but I'm not. I have magick blood so this stuff is my normal. In fact, what is abnormal to me is seeing people all happy and blissfully ignorant about magick. It is real. You would be surprised at how many magickal creatures there are in this world.

Christine nods her head in understanding and laughs, "I would have loved to see your face Jay."

"You see this," as he points between us, "This I don't understand. Magick, shape shifters, and circles you can't see are all new to me." He says a little hurt and mad as he rubs his head. For the first time, he feels way out of his league. I do have to give Jay props though, he is taking it in stride. I would have broken something by now if it were me in his position.

"You know things that drop to the ground when you put two bullets in them, that's what I understand. Not freaky eye changing crap, or little bottles of potion that go boom after it is thrown." He takes a deep breath to calm himself down and to remove the anger from his voice.

"All this crap has got my head spinning like the morning after a night of tequila shots." Jay puts his hands back on the table and proceeds to drum his fingers.

Phenix finally takes this time to speak up. Maybe it's the whole never leave a man down whether you know him or not. The so-called bond that all men share with each other.

"I'm sorry you are going through this Jay, right?" Phenix asks him for confirmation on his name. Jay nods his head yes.

"I can help. First I have been in your shoes when it comes to Sirus. Frankly the only way to deal with it is know she is a bitch. Second I know who is behind these murders." Phenix moves his head around the table looking at each of them. I do the same and can see everyone has the same look on their face after that announcement. *What the hell looks on each of them?*

"What the hell are you talking about Phenix? Why didn't you say anything last night?" I gave him my most annoyed look which falters when he smiles.

"Well for starters I was busy last night." He winks at me and my face goes three shades of red in five seconds.

Oh, he is so going to pay for that. The funny part is I am not one to blush at things easily. He is the only one who has ever been able to make me blush. He has always had that kind of effect on me.

"I'll say," Sirus laughs out loud. I give her my *you can go to hell look.*

"Sorry, been there, done that.", and she laughs again.

"Anyways people and I use that term loosely, we are straying from the matter at hand." I give my full attention to Phenix and the rest of them follow suit.

"Please explain and leave all other matters not involved out." I stress the out part so he gets my meaning.

"Ok, you're right sorry. Anyways I know who is behind this and so do you Elements." He looks at me as if he was trying to send a message telepathically.

"Look I said I may have an idea. There is no concrete evidence to point fingers at anyone. In fact, this whole situation has got me so confused about some things, scared about others, and worried about the rest." I tell him hoping he understands that a more profound explanation is needed.

I'm not dumb, or slow, but I must admit that sometimes my mind doesn't catch as quickly as I would like. In fact, here lately it has reacted just quick enough to keep my ass alive.

"Elements, be quiet for a minute." Phenix says and takes my hand in each of his and brushes a kiss on each knuckle.

I look at him and take a deep breath, "Ok, now what?"

"It's Damon," he says and waits for my reaction. Which he knows is going to drive me straight through the roof, not to mention just his name alone pisses me off and scares me all at the same time.

Damon, all though I like to call him demon. He was the big bad ugly that I had a run in with a few years ago. I haven't seen him or heard from him since he went underground. Now I know why. This is what he was waiting for, enough power to rule.

His main power is he likes to bring chaos where ever he goes. He is nothing but trouble. He thrives on it. He is a psychic vampire and he can mind control you like no other. That is another one of his many powers. He rolls the mind and he can make you do anything he wants.

I barely made it out alive with our last battle, not fight. A fight usually ends in a couple of hours and that's if both parties are equally matched. No with him it was a battle. It lasted months before he decided to go underground.

My, "oh crap meter" just broke. He is one bad ass I was hoping not to face again. In the back of my mind I knew it wasn't over but a girl can hope. I was hoping that he would forget about me. I think he still may be upset with my turning him down because I loved Phenix.

Every single one of us has the potential of getting our asses handed to us. The two that stand to lose the most though are Christine and Phenix. Christine is a sensitive so she and Damon have similar powers. All though she hasn't reached the mind control stage yet, but with practice and help she will be able to roll the mind. That is my hope at least.

Phenix being a panther shape shifter, can easily lose to Damon because he has power over him. You see all psychic vamps when powerful enough have their very own shape shifter that they can control. It is one of the perks so to speak that is if you believe in slavery, which I don't.

Truthfully, I think Damon is or was in love with Phenix, and Phenix has never been attracted to men. I mean Damon is attracted to women too but he just sees it as sex. To him it really doesn't matter who the sex is with, he just loves sex period.

It just dawned on me why Phenix left. To break the bond between psychic vamp and their shape shifter is to disappear and tell no one where you go because then the vamp could get to them through their loved ones by reading their minds. That can either be a pleasant or painful experience. It just depends on what the vampire wants you to feel.

It is no easy task for the shape shifter because it is painful. It's like a drug addict trying to kick the habit and get clean. They go through those withdrawals that causes the body to shake nonstop for days and then the pain comes in overflowing tides and that causes them to throw up. If you are a strong enough shape shifter you will survive the withdrawals and become your own person so to speak with no one having control over, you. Once the bond is broken it cannot happen again.

I look over at Phenix and tears form in my eyes. "I understand now why you left." I lean over to him and place a kiss on his lips. I didn't care who was watching.

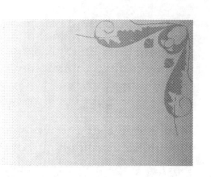

CHAPTER 13

J AY TELLS US THE STATS on the new victim. It turns out she was a witch as well and part of the same Coven. Just like the first victim she was also stabbed to death with her athame. This time the difference was she was a red head. We witches come in all shapes and sizes, color too.

"Like I said she was leaving her meeting or whatever they call them and was attacked from behind. All though this girl defiantly put up a fight. We got scrapings from under her nails. We are just waiting on forensics to run the tests and I'm afraid they are a little behind being a double homicide and all." Jay says looking at each one of us.

As he moves around the table he stops on Phenix, "So you say you know who is behind this?" He gives Phenix the bad cop stare down.

"Yes, it is Damon." Phenix answers without flinching.

"Is this a guess, or do you have some kind of proof?" Jay asks with the same look. I can feel Phenix start getting irritated by Jay's questioning.

"It's fact. Proof I'm working on." Phenix replies as he grabs my hand to hold it.

"Can I ask why you haven't come forward with this and tell the cops what you know?" Jay asks waiting for his explanation.

"Please, it's not like I didn't want too. But except for a few and that may be putting it generously, you cops still have misgivings about us." Phenix tells him. I can see His point of view and it's not because I just slept with him or anything. I know there are a few cops who still treat them like they are animals or a disease. The few that know about us are riding the fence on whether we, meaning magickal beings are good or bad.

Yes, some of us still go into hiding. Everyone probably knows one, just not the magickal part of them. I can totally see his point and the reason why his voice goes taunt every time he talks about cops.

Christine just sits very still and doesn't say anything. She doesn't like confrontation. I can tell she is on edge because she can feel Phenix's powers. It's like a crackling sensation over the skin. Whenever he is on guard his power slips out. I don't think he does it on purpose but I also don't think he realizes that he is doing it.

Like I said Christine can sense all kinds of powers, magick, or whatever you want to call it to be comfortable. She is rubbing her arms up and down like she just got the chills. Sirus doesn't say anything either, she basically just wants to know the facts. Yeah you might think, *oh how thoughtful of her,* nope the facts I'm talking about are when and where and who.

The translation of this is when is the fight, where is the fight, and who are we fighting. Yup, that's it. It's like I said before the girl can't turn down trouble or stay out of it for too long. It's like a drug to her. If someone doesn't start anything after a while she will go out looking for it. *Can I get a Yee-haw!*

Jay is just sitting there trying to make sense of everything and trying to figure out which part if any is true and what proof do we need to take this asshole down.

"Ok, first Jay reel in your cop tude. I realize you are in a tight spot right now being the lead on both cases, but if Phenix gives you a name you can bet on it that he knows what he is talking about. Phenix is not one for guessing or jumping to conclusions. I love and trust you with everything that I hold dear, but we are in this mess together." Jay settles down and starts drumming his fingers on the table. I bet he has the game rock bands for his Xbox at home.

"If Damon is behind this which I have no doubt that he isn't than we are all going to need to work together to get out of this mess. Jay, you don't know him and you didn't know me when I had my run in with Damon, but I am telling you he is not someone to take lightly. Not even a little bit."

Jay gives me his full attention because he knows I'm speaking the truth. I always have and I always will.

"Christine, you and I met shortly after the fall out. It was about two weeks later and I was still trying to recover from the battle. I almost died that night. In fact, I still don't know why I didn't, but I am glad I did survive. Now let's stop squabbling and come up with a plan." They all nod their heads in agreement with me.

"He has already killed two witches, and while I did not see him I know he was the one behind the attack at Christine's. My guess and I hope I'm wrong is that he will come after me or Phenix next. Especially if he knows you are back in town." I look at Phenix and he nods his head.

Christine gets up for more coffee. She will be pissing a river later with all the coffee she has drank. She could probably piss out a latte right now if you asked. Not to mention caffeine over load. She will be up all night and then crash and burn in the early morning. I had to get up from the table to stretch my legs. Whenever I get stressed I have to move around or my muscles will tighten up on me, like they were starting to now. My mind is going a mile a minute as I look around the table at each one's face. I can't help but think, *what if I let them down? Or worse they get killed because of my past?*

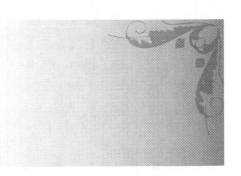

CHAPTER 14

I AM SITTING AT THE TABLE again tapping my foot when I look over at Phenix and then the others who are here. "I can't believe that son of a bitch. That asshole is going down." I screamed at the top of my lungs to release tension.

I get up and start pacing my kitchen floor again. I should have toned thighs by now with all the pacing I'm doing. I am so angry right now that not even the touch of Phenix's hand on my arm can calm me down. I am scared because Damon has the power to kill every single one of us here. I don't know if I can win against him without the possibility of losing one or more of them. I throw my hands out and white flames shoot from them and hit a glass on the counter causing it to explode.

"Shit." Jay says as he covers his head, and Christine ducks. I just stare in shock at the glass dust on the counter.

"What the heck was that?" Jay asks and stares at me. I can see in his eyes that his mind is dancing with everything and he doesn't know how to take this new power of mine. He almost looks scared of me. Hell, I'm scared of me right now. *Elements, what the hell was that? Already knowing the answer to that question. My mind is unable to process; I am becoming the weapon that I was told about from my grandparents.* I just stare down at my hands as if I had ten fingers on each of them.

Phenix grabs me by the shoulders, "Elements, we will win this. We will all stick together and we will win. We will put him down." I just look at him in amazement. *How the hell does he always know what I'm thinking? I wish I could be that perceptive.*

"What if you are wrong Phenix?" My hands begin to shake. The adrenalin just pumping through me, and the fear.

He grabs a hold of my hands, "First let's put these down, referring to my hands. We don't need that, as he looks over at the counter, to happen again. I like my head where it's at thank you very much. I think the others will agree about their own head". I just smile a little as I let go of my anger.

Everyone is staring at my hands and I start to feel uncomfortable with all the attention. Great now I have my own friends afraid of me. Time to bring Damon back to the topic of discussion instead of my new flame throwing power. I so need to call my Nana tonight. Hopefully she can give me some answers or hell maybe the Divine will if I call on them enough. I mean after all it is their prophecies that I have been told about since I was a little girl and came into my powers at the age of thirteen.

"What if he is better than us? I can't lose. Not to him, I just can't." I return to my chair and sit putting my head on the table. I don't know what else to do right now. My mind is being an ass and putting visions and images of my friends' dead and covered in blood. It can't happen. I won't let it.

"This needs to be over and I mean like yesterday over". Christine says as she takes a sip of her coffee. I know she is scared. I'm scared of a lot of things. For one scared of losing my friends. Two I'm scared of losing Phenix again now that he is back in my life. The third failing and dying before I can show them how much they mean to me, and how my life wouldn't be much of one without them in it.

"I agree Christine". Jay says, "We need to figure out where this Damon is and have him pay for his crimes."

"Jay, there is no arresting him. If I get a hold of him I'm going to straight up kill him, and that's that. No way am I letting him get away. Now I know you might have to arrest me since I just made a threat of killing someone in front of you, but it's going to happen regardless." I look at Jay so he knows and understands that I mean what I say.

"What are you talking about? I didn't hear anything." He smiles at me and gives me a wink.

Phenix starts fidgeting I think he is uncomfortable with mine and Jay's relationship. I don't think he believes men and women can be friends and not be sleeping together.

Sirus who has been sitting silently the whole time finally speaks up. "I don't know what the hell you guys are talking about. I just want to know where this Damon is so I can fight. Hell, that's the only reason I came. I don't really care about any of yall's life or what you do with them, or who you do." She looks over at me when she says her last statement.

I forgot just how much of a bitch she really is. That's fine with me because nice is not going to keep us alive. We need straight up bitch mode, that's what will keep us alive. Damon is straight up a fight to the death kind of thing. There is no in between. *Can I get a yee-haw?*

CHAPTER 15

PHENIX SAID HE WAS GOING out to scout for information. Whatever the hell that means. Jay had to get back to the station to do more paper work on the second woman. Christine was going shopping. She said all this crap was getting to her. Shopping is her way to cope with stress. She will probably buy herself a pair of red thigh high boots now and complain when she has to run in them. *That's my girl.* Sirus said she was just going out. That will not end well, I just know it. That can mean anything.

So, I decided to have some me time. I needed to go commune with the goddess and have her help me find an answer out of this. One that has us all still among the land of the living. I also need to get answers about this new power I have attained and whether Damon is the big evil that I am to use it against. The evil that all witches have been taught about since our birth.

I step out of my house for a little fresh air and to replenish my inner strength. I was so going to need it, especially when the fighting starts. As soon as I step out I am hit with one hell of a psychic hit. I fall backwards hitting my head on the steps and dizziness consumes me. The pain is so strong it's shooting through my head causing me to almost vomit. I see little white lights dancing before my eyes.

I take a deep breath trying to listen. I open my eyes slowly and start scanning my yard trying to figure out who and where it came from. My eyes land on a familiar face, not one I know but one I have seen. I can't place where yet but I'm betting she's connected to Damon. My head clearing up a little more I start to rise. As I adjust my eyes the name comes to me... Raven.

I remember her now. She is one of his harlots from his harem. He doesn't really have a harem, what I mean is she is one of the many women who will do whatever he asks including sharing his bed. I was never big on the sharing thing. After all I was an only child and I didn't play well with others.

"Hello Elements, Damon sends his regards." She says so sarcastically that it must be her first language.

"Ahh, Raven I see you are still playing second best." I tell her matching her sarcasm with my own.

"I see you are still wasting your powers on the side of good." Raven says flipping her long red hair across her shoulders.

"Every chance I get. I see you are still doing Damon's bidding." I say mocking her same movement with the hair. I never did understand why girls did that. I mean really what is it with the hair flip? I was always taught that it's a flirting move.

I send a strong psychic hit towards her and she only staggers a bit. *Oh crap! What the hell is going on? I am in so much trouble.* I am normally stronger than this, hell most times I'm unstoppable. Now I know my powers are seriously needing a recharge.

Come on Elements think of something. You can't let this bitch get the best of you. First I need to calm down. Never let your enemy see or smell fear. Believe me it does have a distinct smell to it. If you give in, you will lose. Just as I was about to say a spell a strong force grabs hold of my throat. It felt like a hand squeezing me and cutting off my air supply. I reached up on instinct and can't grab anything. *Duh, Elements it's magick!*

I can feel the tug of darkness consuming me and luring me to sleep. I try and fight it but I can't. My body starts giving in and my eyes slowly close. Right before I slip into unconsciousness I hear her parting words.

"You and your friends are going to die. Damon has become very strong that even you and your magick can't stop him. Even now while you slip into darkness there is a plan in motion."

I hear nothing more and fall into the dark abyss.

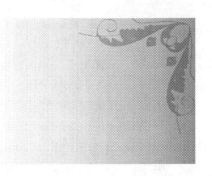

CHAPTER 16

J AY AND CHRISTINE FOUND ME crumbled on the steps of my porch. In the distance, I can hear my name being called. "Elements, Elements."

My eyes slowly open and all I see is a blurry face hovering above mine. My eyes now become focused and I realize it was Jay and he was gently shaking me to wake me up. The sun reflects off his dark colored hair. It has a sparkle to it, but I will never tell him that. I stare into his brown eyes and I can see that he is concerned. I give him what I hope is a *I'm ok smile,* but failed.

"Hey Jay." Just a whisper slipping pass my lips and he tries to help me to a sitting position.

Pain instantly shoots through my head and I close my eyes immediately to fight off the dizziness. Finally, able to open my eyes more I can see Christine looking around my yard like she is searching for the source of the magick that was used. She can still feel the energy of the powers that were used here few minutes ago. At least I hope it was just a few minutes. I have no idea how long I was out.

After satisfying herself that there was no immediate threat she walks over to Jay and helps him help me to my feet. Finally, on my feet I have only one thought, *damn no ritual today.*

I just got my ass kicked and that's all I can think about. I never said I was the smartest witch around.

"Seriously Elements, what the hell happened?" Christine says as she puts an arm around my waist to help me walk. She was always like that. Concerned for my safety. I'm the ultimate weapon and she's worried about me.

"What happened was Raven?" I tell her. They don't know her just a piece of my past that's kicking my butt.

"Didn't you like teach her or something?" Jay asks.

"No, not really. She was just a young girl who got mixed up with the wrong people. I was just trying to help her with her powers. I guess Damon was a more exciting ride. He has messed with her mind so much that she wouldn't know right from wrong even if it was a blinking light." I guess that's what they mean when they say *the road to hell is paved with good intentions.*

"So, what was that, a surprise visit saying thanks for everything?" Christine says pissed off.

"Yup, you could say that." I tell her as we walk back into the house. My mind just keeps playing on repeat of her parting words. *Damon is even more powerful than even your magick and that there was a plan already in motion.*

I sit down at the kitchen table finally able to concentrate without my head feeling like a jack hammer. "We are in some serious trouble here and I'm talking chest level". I say as I put my hand up in union.

"What the hell does that mean?" They both say together.

"It's not a game anymore. Damon is out for blood. Not just any blood but my blood. He will stop at nothing until he achieves what he sets out to do. That means everyone is in danger." I say in a shaky voice so unlike my own strong one I'm used to hearing.

I take the ice pack Christine has prepared for me and place it at the back of my head. The cool contact was instant relief to the headache trying to form. She looks at me and I already know what she's going to ask, but I play dumb and let her ask anyways.

"Elements what is going on with you and your powers? This is so not you. You would have knocked that girl out with a flick of your wrist." She looks at me as if I know the answer already. Which I don't. I have no freakin idea what the hell is going on with me or my powers, but they are sooo letting me down.

I wonder if maybe because of my newest power that the rest of them are going haywire until I get used to it and it finds its place inside of me. "It's just all this crap. I haven't had time to re-energize them or me. Being magickal doesn't make you invincible. It just makes you harder to kill. If you don't take care of them by recharging so to speak, they become worthless."

53

"Well than you better go find the energizer bunny and recharge, because this crap ain't funny." Jay says.

"Yeah and neither are you. Besides it doesn't work like that, butthead." I smile at him anyways.

I know sarcasm is one of his weapons and he must really be worried to use it during a time of crisis. "I have to stay in touch with the four elements to keep my powers up to par. Which of course is what I was trying to do this morning before I was so rudely interrupted." I start rubbing my head again.

"Al right ya'll this is some serious stuff; could we not make freakin jokes." Christine says as she gets up and goes to the coffee pot.

I can tell everyone is scared weather they admit it or not. You can't be human or normal if you weren't afraid when it's this close to home. Well I mean I'm not truly human but Jay is. It's kind of funny, magickal creatures bleed, cry, and sleep just like humans do, but the law still won't classify us as humans. Now how messed up is that when you still have prejudice in this generation?

I would love to see people's faces when they find out that their neighbor or coworker is some form of a magickal being. I bet their mouth would drop open wide enough to catch flies and choke on them. I apologize I still get a little pissy when I see how we get discriminated against.

I reached out to squeeze Christine's hand. Just to let her know with touch what my voice can't say. She returns the touch to let me know she feels the same way. She trusts me to get us out of this mess. She knows I will do my damndest to keep us alive. *Gee no pressure here, Yee-haw!*

She gets up from the table and gets some coffee because it's done brewing. She turns to me and says, "We kick this Damon's ass and kill him and then we get to have margaritas, deal?" I laugh and she smiles at me.

"Why can't it ever be Corona, or any beer for that matter? Hell, even Jack or Jim will do. Why does it always have to be margaritas? Why the hell does Jose always win?" Jay says with a little boy crushed voice.

He is trying to lighten the mood because in the back of his mind one of us or all of us could be dead soon. Christine and I laugh at him, "Fine it can be whatever you want it to be as long as we kick ass ok and win." We tell him. With that he gets a big cheesy grin on his face. Like a kid who just threw a tantrum and still got his way.

CHAPTER 17

W E FIGURED WE NEEDED TO get our game on and bring Damon down and soon. I was not going to let him get away with killing those two witches as well as what he has done to Phenix in the past. I'll be damned if he gets another witch. We have come up with the beginnings of a plan but sadly we are missing the middle and the end.

I was in the kitchen making some potions for us which will increase our personal powers. I can't make one for Jay because he doesn't have magick blood, but I did bless a talisman that will keep him from getting his mind controlled by Damon. I don't want Damon picking on him first because of his small flaw of no magick and being human. I also blessed a couple of his bullets. They will not be able to kill the vamps but it will cause some serious damage that won't heal right away. In the end, we will be doing a lot of hand to hand and maybe foot to mouth contact.

Phenix comes up behind me and snakes his arms around my waist. "So, how's the head?" He asks.

"It's fine. Nothing a little aspirin and magick can't fix."

"You know Elements; it could have been worse. How the hell could you let your magick get so low? That's not like you." Phenix says scolding me like I'm a child and did something wrong. I hate hearing that kind of tone in his voice. It was stupid of me to let my powers slip, but it's like I did it on purpose.

"I know. The last few days, not to mention hours there hasn't been any time."

Hello, have you forgotten two dead witches, the attack at Christine's house, your surprise visit, Raven coming by to say hello, but of course I don't say any of this because he is just concerned, he doesn't deserve it at least not yet.

I stir the potion and watch it go from black to green which means it is done. This one is for me. It is an Earth potion because that is my element. I can use the other three elements but Earth is mine and I can control it way better than the others, but it doesn't mean I won't use them if I have too. I pick up the pan and pour it into a little bottle and place it with the others on the counter. There is a sky blue one which is Phenix's because his element is air. Christine's is a deep ocean blue because Water is her element. The red one goes to Sirus because her element is fire.

All the potions are cooling in their bottles, because they still have a few hours before they will be ready. I don't want us to drink them too soon because the effects only last twenty-four hours than boom we are back to just our normal strength.

"So, have we gotten any further with the plan then we were before?" Jay asks loudly as he walks through the door into the house.

Phenix let go of me because he hates showing any affection in front of people especially a man. I guess to him it shows weakness and you know a man cannot will not show weakness if it can be helped.

Jay walks into the kitchen and looks around, "Where is everyone? Is it even safe to be separated since we have all had our little episode with this Damon fellow?" He walks over to the fridge and grabs a Mountain Dew. I can't stand the stuff but he loves it, so I keep it stocked up for him. Just like how I keep coffee on hand for Christine and little ole me.

"Well Christine I'm sure is out picking the perfect butt kicking outfit, she should be here soon. Sirus is asleep in the guest room, she was out late. Which reminds me have you heard anything about a fight in a place called The Club?" I ask Jay as I turn around and face him.

"Yeah, some third shifters were talking about it when I came in this morning. Why?" He asks as he squints his eyes at me with the look of *what do you know.*

"Nothing. Just mark it up as a typical night at the club." I give him my most sincere smile. He just rolls his eyes at me. Jay turns from me and takes a seat at the kitchen table. Phenix and I join him as we exchange looks.

Jay catches this brief exchange of glances, "What?" he asks hating the way he feels already.

"Phenix and I have been talking and we believe we have come up with a way to get rid of Damon for good." I pause so I can let that sink in before continuing and to let Jay get a sip of soda.

"But…I Know there is a but in this scenario, because with you Elements there is always a but, and most of the time I don't like them." Jay says matter of fact and just a little annoyed.

"Well I was looking at some of my magick books and there is a ritual we can do, and we meaning Christine, Phenix, Sirus, and myself."

"Why can't I be a part of it?" he asks nervous about the answer. I know he is nervous because I can feel it, and if I can feel it, I know Phenix can taste it.

"You have to be of magickal descent to perform it, and pretty powerful to survive it." I say the end in a slight whisper but loud enough to be heard still.

"Uh huh, and there's the but I was talking about." Jay jumps up from his chair mad. He starts pacing the kitchen floor.

Jay is pacing back and forth mumbling stuff under his breath that I couldn't make out and to tell you the truth I probably didn't want too.

I get up from my chair and reach out for Jay's arm, "First stop pacing, you are giving me a headache." He looks at me and I give him a smile. Phenix starts moving in his chair uncomfortably. He hates seeing emotions, any emotions.

"I'm not saying we are going to do it right now, but the option is out there, especially if it turns out not in our favor. I don't want you to get hurt Jay and besides there is a forty percent chance we can survive this ritual."

"Well damn Elements why didn't you say so. Hell, forty percent that's something to bank on with sixty percent chance you can die yeah, let's do it." Jay says sarcastically as he crosses his arms in front of his chest.

Just great now he is going to be stubborn. I hate when he acts like that. He becomes like a child getting ready to throw a tantrum. This is where he and Phenix are the same. I'm beginning to think it is all men.

I give up and roll my eyes and turn back to the kitchen table and sit down. Phenix and I begin to talk again about the ritual. "Is there anything special you need to do or special tools you need to perform this?" Phenix asks. In the back ground, we hear the front door slam from Jay leaving.

CHAPTER 18

I WAS IN MY ROOM GETTING ready for the annual policeman's ball, something I have been doing for the last couple of years. Jay asks me to go with him to pretend to be his girlfriend because there is a woman on the force who has a major crush on him. He thinks it's easier to pretend you are taken than hurt her feelings.

I was just putting the finishing touches of my make up on when Phenix came in. "Where are you going all dressed up?"

I look at him in the mirror and smile, "Wouldn't you like to know?" I let out a laugh because of the look on his face, even though he has a small smile on his lips.

"I go to the ball every year with Jay so he can fend off all the single ladies on the force with him."

"Why doesn't he just tell them he's not interested?" Phenix asks as he starts to massage my shoulders.

I lean back into him and close my eyes. I can feel the stress slipping away with each rub. He has always had great hands. Sometimes I find myself doing things just so we can touch. He is American Indian so he has this year-round tan that looks great. Which sucks, because I can't seem to tan to save my life anymore. Now days all I do is burn, but it does not stop me from going to the beach. I can't swim but I do love walking the beach bare footed, and feeling the sun on me.

"I guess he doesn't want to hurt their feelings. He really is just a nice guy."

"That is so stupid.", he says as his hands travel lower down my back. I feel his hand on my bottom and I open one eye and look at him in the mirror.

"Behave Phenix. I don't have time for this."

He leans down and whispers in my ear, "Stay home and I'll take you to your own ball." He says with a mischievous look as he lays feather light kisses on my neck.

I instantly get goosebumps and a sigh escapes my lips. My body begins to react to his touches. If it were possible to pass out from sheer pleasure, I would so be on the floor.

"Phenix please." I plead with him because my body is ready to give in and give up. He pulls back and let's go so abruptly that both my eyes open.

"Now what's wrong?" I ask because I'm confused about his behavior.

"Are you sure he isn't after anything more than friendship?" He asks me and I can see that he is serious because it's in his eyes. I turn to look at the ground to cover up my smile. It's nice to have someone who gets a little jealous.

"Are you serious? Really? Yes, I am sure. There is nothing but friendship between us. We are more like brother and sister than anything else." I walk over to him and place my hand gently on his face, so that he has no choice but to look at me. "I promise you are the only one I want." I give him a kiss that leaves us both breathless. He leaned into me and pulled me so close and tight that I could hardly breathe. Just when things started to get a little hot, "Knock, knock"

I look down to the ground, "Come in."

The door opens and Jay walks in. He exchanges looks with Phenix before saying anything. I know he is still upset about the ritual, but he knows if there is another way to get rid of Damon I will find it.

"Wow, Elements you look great." He gives me a genuine smile. One that hasn't really been on his face since this whole thing started.

"Thank you. I just want to say that for the record these heels are already killing my feet." I lift the hem of my gown so they could see my four inch black stilettos. Jay lets out a whistle so loud that I just laugh. Phenix was just standing there like someone pissed in his cheerios. *He'll get over it.*

He gives Jay a dead stare, "Do you really think this is wise going to the ball with all the excitement we have had the last couple of days?" He crosses his arms over his chest.

"Look Phenix I understand ok. I really do. I promise nothing will happen to her in my care. Can we please just call it a truce between us?" Jay asks holding his hand out for a shake.

Phenix grabs it and gives it a brief shake. "Ok, truce but if anything happens I better get a phone call. Deal?"

Jay looks him in the eye, "Deal." They both let go at the same time.

Phenix turns to me and closes the gap between us with a few strides of his long legs. He pulls me in hard and gives me one of those kisses that is meant to stake his claim. I felt like I was getting pissed on like a dog does when he marks his territory. I didn't know whether to laugh or get annoyed so I just let it be.

All three of us leave the bedroom and head to the kitchen so I can get my purse off the table. It's hard to be truly comfortable in a gown when you are wearing enough weapons to start a war. I have three potions strapped to my leg in a garter plus a blade. I am leaving the gun home because it's too big for my purse.

Jay holds his elbow to me, "Our chariot awaits my dear." He says in a mock British accent.

"Why thank you kind sir." I respond back in my own imitation of the British accent.

I can feel Phenix's power flare up because of jealousy. "Stop it Phenix." He rolls his eyes but pulls his power back in. Jay is oblivious of what just happened because he has no sense of magick.

"I won't be home too late, and I promise we will pick up where we left off." I say to Phenix and give him a wink. He smiles in return and shows me promises of his own with his eyes. We walk out the front door and there is a black limo waiting in the driveway.

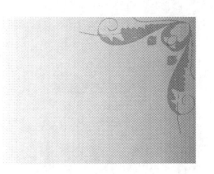

CHAPTER 19

W E HAVE BEEN HERE AT the ball for about an hour in a half and I'm trying to fain off my yawning. Jay is sitting next to me shooting the breeze with some of his buddies. One of the women at the table who likes him is sitting across from him hanging on to his every word. *Barf!* I mean really can you be more obvious. She's laughing at all his jokes and half of them aren't even that funny. It doesn't even seem to bother her that his "girlfriend" is sitting next to him watching everything.

I hear some commotion at the front entrance of the ballroom and I look up. I squint my eyes trying to figure out who is causing it. It's not like I would know anyways; these aren't my people. I look anyways after all it's better than listening to the conversation at the table, or watching the girl make googly eyes at Jay. Just as my eyes land on the new person who walked in I stare in shock. *Are you freakin kidding me? Really? Crap, shit just became real.*

I start tapping Jay on his shoulder, "Jay, Jay," I whisper to him.

"What Elements," he answers with concern. He wonders what's wrong.

"Do you know who just walked in the door?" I ask him with all seriousness.

Jay looks over at the entrance to register whom I'm talking about. "Yeah, that's the guest of honor. He gave the department a huge donation and I mean huge. A million dollars huge. Why" He looks back at me and he can see my oh crap look on my face and he becomes serious.

"No Jay, that is freakin Damon, and let me tell you that money is almost all dirty. It's drug money and whatever else he has his teeth into. I'm betting it's almost all illegal as well. We need to get the hell out of here and I mean like now. We need to get back to my house."

My adrenaline starts pumping, and it gets hard to breathe for a minute. *Relax, breathe in... breathe out... Center yourself,* my mind tells me.

We get up from the table as I fain a migraine so we can leave. We almost make it out without any interruption until I look back and see Damon's eyes on me. *Oh, crap!* And before I even had time to put my psychic guard up I felt him dipping into my mind and began rolling it. I start walking over to him against my will. In the distant I can hear my name being called.

"Elements, Elements what the hell is wrong with you?" I can feel myself being shaked.

I blink my eyes and settle on Jay who is in front of me looking into my eyes. I see the worried expression on Jay's face.

"Son of a ... he rolled me. The vamp was screwing with my mind." I shake my head side to side clearing the little bit of fuzz that was still lingering there in my mind. "Jay, we are so in trouble."

"What do we do? We can't very well start a fight here in the middle of hundreds of cops, detectives, and commissioners." Jay states like it was even an option I would consider.

"Jay take my cell phone and call Phenix." I handed it to him. "I'm going over there to stall Damon on whatever he has planned. I know he has one because he is not here for the entertainment."

Jay nods his head and goes to the wall to place the call. I walk over to Damon and he has a big fat smile on his face.

"Elements, what a pleasant surprise seeing you here. You look beautiful tonight." He says with the lilt in his voice that starts the mind rolling. I can tell he is trying to control my mind with his voice. Even though it sounds as pure and smooth as silk I know it is filled with nothing but evil.

"Damon", I say trying to control my anger and not spit out my words like venom. "You ever try that crap again on me and I swear to you that you will regret it." I give him my most sincere sarcastic, don't mess with me kind of smile.

Jay reaches my side and puts his arm on me as if he was protecting me from harm. "They are on their way." He says as he looks at Damon. He stares back at Jay and I can't help but smile because I know he is trying to roll Jay's mind. Jay suspects as much and pulls out the dragon charm I gave him.

"Yeah, I don't think so Damon." He puts it back in his shirt pocket.

"Awe, Elements, you take all the fun out of everything. What do you plan to do? Start a war here in the middle of the police men's ball?" Damon says as he spreads his arm out and looks around scanning the room. I see him give a slight nod to someone as if he was signaling them.

I feel a slight pressure on my back. I know the feel. I can even see the object in my mind. Every curve, every detail of it. Once you have had a gun on you it is not something you will soon forget.

"What do you want me to do now?" asked to person at my back. I know that voice. *Think Elements, think.* Than it clicks, it's the bimbo from our table that was drooling on Jay's every word, and laughing at all his jokes. She was a plant. She was told to come here in hopes of cornering us for a surrender. *Bitch!*

"This whole thing is a trap Jay." As I was thinking of possible reasons why Damon would plan this, the answer hits me like a lightning bolt. Phenix. Damon wants him, and we just lead him here. *Gee honey, I'm sorry. It was a trap. He wants you and I gave you to him, but hey I love you. What a freakin great girlfriend I am.*

"Don't even think about calling him back," Damon says and he motions with his hand for Jay to put the cell phone back in his pocket.

"Why can't you leave him alone and let him be Damon?" I ask him pure anger in my voice.

CHAPTER 20

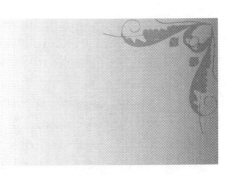

P HENIX HAS JUST WALKED THROUGH the doors and he heads straight for us. I try and plead with him with my eyes but he is ignoring the warning. *I'll be damned if I lose him now that he has returned into my life.* That being my last thought I go at a full charge at Damon. He is taken by complete surprise and hits the ground. Before anyone can pull their guns, I throw a potion and hear Damon scream in pain.

"Like I said Damon, it won't kill you but it hurts like hell doesn't it. It's like being doused with holy water." In the last remnants of his scream I say a quick spell that freezes the room.

"Ok guys, we have five minutes to get the hell out of here." We take off running through the doors and outside to the limo waiting curb side. We jump into the back and I yell out for the driver to take us back to my house.

Back at the house we are sitting around the kitchen table trying to figure out how we are going to survive this. That was just a little too close for comfort if you get my meaning. You don't usually get to be that close to Damon and live. We were just dang lucky. He wasn't expecting that kind of retaliation in a room full of law officials. He didn't know I was going to be there and he sure as heck didn't know I always have a plan on getting out. Call it precaution or paranoid, either way we are still here. Yee haw!

"Elements, how the heck did you hide those bottles with the dress you were wearing?" Jay asks totally surprised. I mean it was a pretty tight gown. "That dress was so tight I didn't even see the outlines of them." He says to me. "What else do you have on?" He asks just out of curiosity.

I stand up from my chair and pull out two knives, and a blade about six inches long. "A witch is always prepared." He lets out a loud whistle, which caused everyone else to bust out laughing.

"Remind me to never ever piss you off." Jay states as he sits down and stares at the weapons.

"Oh sweetie, that's nothing. You should have seen what I was packing last year." Jay just looks at me with complete and utter shock on his face.

"How did you get passed the metal detectors at the front entrance?" He looks at me.

"Oh that, easy. I just said a small deactivation spell right before we walked through the doors. They kicked back on after we were through them." He just laughs trying to ease the strain that was building right between his shoulder blades.

Sirus takes that time to enter from somewhere in the back of the house, "What did I miss?" She asks looking at each of us. We all just laugh because none of us could find the words that would make it sound remotely close to the truth.

"Seriously guys, don't leave me hangin." She begs with her eyes as she takes the last vacant seat at the table.

"Nothing really. A bunch of cops dressed up. Lousy music, a run in with Damon, and not very good food." I tell her.

"Whoa, what Damon?" She asks.

"Yes, it turns out he was the guest of honor." I tell her and see complete surprise take over her face.

"How the heck does that happen? I mean Damon is as bad as bad can be." She says still not believing what she heard.

"Well in today's world money talks and gets you recognition. Despite on how you got it or where it came from." I tell her shrugging my shoulders.

I can feel a migraine coming on. It always happens like that. When you use magick it will use you back. There is always a price to pay when dealing with magick. Christine just arrived so we could go over our plan.

"What makes you so sure Damon won't attack tonight?" Christine asks.

"Elements wounded him pretty bad with one of her potions. We are good tonight. He will be healed by tomorrow night though. I know if it were me I would so be pissed I got whooped by a girl." Jay says and laughs.

Everyone will be staying at my house tonight. After the rest of them go to bed Jay and I will talk more about the plan and strategy. I tell him more about the ritual in detail so he understands that this is as serious as it comes. Metaphysics is not something to take lightly. I also told him what he had to do. I know he will fight me on this until the very end but it can't be helped. He must understand the power that will have to be drawn up to kill Damon. I also have to get him to understand that there is a chance the we, the we being Phenix, Sirus, Christine, and myself may not survive it.

This ritual is so old that the last time it was used was when witches were still hiding from those who called themselves inquisitionists who were burning women and children at the stake. That is how old this ritual is. That is also the reason why Jay needs to understand how important everything and everyone involved is.

I am not looking forward to doing this. I mean I don't want to die and I don't want to see those I care about die. This is it. The last chance to get rid of Damon forever. However, there is a bright side though, we do have a forty percent chance of surviving this. *See not all bad.*

CHAPTER 21

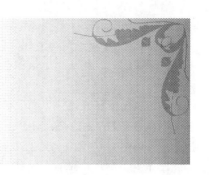

W E ARE IN MY KITCHEN and it just turned dark outside. The street lights have come on and the moon was in her full glory. Christine was stirring a pot when she stopped and looked at me. "They're here."

"Ok you guys just remember what we discussed. We will put an end to this once and for all." I tell them as a pep talk to prepare everyone. *How do you stay positive when you know there is a chance that one or all of us could die tonight? I look at each of them and pray that we all make it out.*

"Remember do whatever you have too to get them in the back yard." I look at them and can feel everyone's adrenaline climaxing into a huge power boost.

I can feel Phenix's power coming in full and strong. His panther just lurking on the inside of him pacing. Christine has a bright glow about her which is new. I have never seen it during any of four other battles we have had. Sirus is calling to the strengths of all cats. I am just balancing my inner elements. I must maintain that especially now with the new power of flame throwing residing in me. I look out of my window and see Damon talking to his group of dark warriors.

"Everyone know your target. Luke, you go after the sensitive, Storm take the cat Sirus. Kala, you go after Phenix and don't kill him just wear him down. I want him back alive, do you understand?" She nods her head instead of answering because she was filled with jealousy over Damon's feelings for Phenix.

Damon understands that he has an un natural relationship or feelings for Phenix but he doesn't care. Phenix has always been able to sense his deepest darkest secrets. "Stephen, you take care of the detective, make him wish he never heard of magick and creatures like us. I want you to make it slow and painful at first then take him out. I want Elements to suffer with the pain of losing him. She has a bond with the detective. I will take on the witch herself. Everyone clear on what they have to do?" Damon looks at each of his members and they in turn nod in understanding.

In the house, we are all just taking deep breaths and feeling the power of each other. "Ok, get them in the center of the circle and I will close it before they even know what hit them. Christine, you will have to be more in tune to your power so you can feel it. Phenix, Sirus you will be able to see the circle. Jay I made you a potion... It doesn't taste the greatest but if you drink it you will be able to see the magick." I look him directly in the eyes.

Jay just looks back at me because this is where he will argue with me about altering himself. He has a strong opinion about it. He doesn't believe in doing that for any cause. No drugs, no magick.

"Elements I told you, no potion. I already don't like the plan. You don't even know if this ritual will work. Not to mention the whole part about possibly dying." *I knew it. See argument!* I look at him and see something flash in his eyes, like he wanted to say something but the image was gone in a blink of an eye. Undisclosed feelings, unspoken words. At least that was the feeling I got from that look.

"Jay I understand that you don't want to take it and I will respect that and not pressure you, but can you at least put it in your pocket just in case you change your mind?" He holds his hand out for the dark purple bottle.

He holds the bottle up into the light of the kitchen and then looks at Christine and I, "Only if the fat lady starts to sing." I nod to him and shrug my shoulders to Christine with the unspoken message, *I tried.*

"That's better than a straight up no." I give him a sincere smile.

I could cast a spell and make him drink the potion, but that is a no no. At least it is for a white witch, because we believe in freedom of choice and I respect him enough to go with his wishes. That is the one drawback in the witch world, all these powers and spells and you can't use them even if you know it would be better for the person. Not without permission.

CHAPTER 22

J AY IS STILL LOOKING AT the bottle shaking it from side to side gently. "Elements what is in it?"

"You know just the typical ingredients, wing of bat, …eye of newt… blood of dragon." His eyes go as big as saucers and his face turns very pale with a green tint to it. Phenix and Sirus are chuckling in the background. I would to be laughing if this wasn't such a serious matter. Serious or not that doesn't stop Christine who just busted out laughing. Yes, it was mean to tease him but if you can't laugh in the face of danger what good is it?

"I'm kidding Jay." I look at him and see his face slowly change back to normal. "It's all natural ingredients except for dragon's blood that is in there. That's where the bad taste comes from. It is only a drop though." I smile at him as he gives me a very irritated look.

"Fat lady.", He says as he puts the bottle in his pocket.

"Got it, fat lady, understood." I hold in a small laugh.

He knows this is no game. Real life, real people and fear crosses his face for a moment. He shakes it off like nothing. "Well then I guess my butt better stay in the middle." He laughs trying to loosen up some. *This will be the first magickal fight Jay will be a part of.*

"I don't want either of you getting to close to the walls, understand?" I look at Jay and Christine, waiting for the nod they understand the stakes here.

"I will be the only one safe from the shocks because it's my blood, my circle."

I look at Phenix and Sirus, "I'm not worried about you two when it comes to the shock because it won't affect you guys, besides a little tingly sensation when you get close to it." They nod their heads and let me know they understood.

"Keep in mind the circle is twelve by twelve, so it will seem a little tight with all of us and them inside. This will work to our advantage because they won't even know until it's too late." With that we all take a moment to call on our inner strengths and prepare for battle. I look at everyone and they understand the seriousness of this. It has settled in their eyes and their bodies have all taken on the extra power. I give each one of them their potion and we all drink them together. The effect is immediate. Our glows become brighter and stronger and our personal powers are boosted to the highest possible level without being part of the Divine.

"Ready?" Everyone looks at each other for a silent goodbye and the pleasure of fighting together.

"Let's do this!" and I open the door.

CHAPTER 23

I OPEN THE FRONT DOOR AND within seconds we are all air born flying back into the house landing about eight feet from the door.

"Damn!", we get back up onto our feet.

"The assholes aren't even waiting!" Jay says pissed off.

"That's it. If they want to play let's freakin play!" I look at them and make sure everyone is alright.

"This is what we are going to do, just start running your butts off and head for the back yard. Let's make them chase us." They all understand exactly what I mean.

"Let's get them inside the circle and I will close it up after the last one enters and then it will be Game on. Are we clear?"

No words were needed. We all take off like our pants are on fire and run as fast as we can to the back yard. I already have my athame in my hand so I can close the circle as soon as Christine gives me the signal. We can hear them running right behind us. No need to look over our shoulders. I'm trying to keep my breathing normal so I don't get light headed. *So far so good.*

They are practically on top of us. Damon was spitting out some nasty words about us and complaining.

"Elements I have never run from a fight in my entire life." Jay yells as he starts panting.

"Don't think of it as running from a fight, think of it as stacking the odds in our favor!" I yell back at him.

Christine is not saying anything. She already knows the drill. She just keeps concentrating on her feet so she doesn't trip up. *In a pair of lovely red thigh highs. Nice. That's my girl!*

We cross the circle and wait to try to catch our breaths. Damon and his crew cross over and Christine yells out, "Now!"

I cut my hand on the inside of my palm and let the red warm liquid flow to the ground to close the circle. My blood hits the ground and a loud buzzing noise is heard by everyone, well except Jay he is oblivious to the sound. Right then I knew he still had the potion in his pocket instead of drinking it. I thought he would have after the first hit back at the house.

Christine can feel the power of the circle, and looks at Jay who is just standing there. She to realized that he did not drink the potion. We both cross our fingers and hope for the best. I say a quick prayer for Jay, and then I hear Damon curse my name, "You Bitch!"

CHAPTER 24

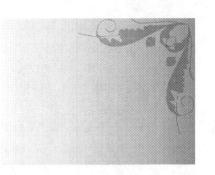

DAMON IS STARING AT ME with the angriest, pissed off death look I have ever seen. "I didn't take you as a cheater Elements."

"I'm not cheating, just evening out the playing field." I say to him as I prepare to fight him one on one.

Damon sends the first hit knocking me to the ground. I hit it hard but I don't feel the pain and I get back up dusting myself off.

"Let the games begin!" I say and throw my own hit back at him.

Storm starts to send one towards Jay and Christine yells out in warning, "Jay!" and she points in the direction.

Jay takes off running, "I usually don't fight girls, but for you I will make an exception." And the force of his running tackle picks her up off her feet and knocks her down flat on her back. "From what I understand you should be used to this position." He says with a sarcastic sneer.

Luke tries to sneak up behind Jay and Christine takes off after him. She pushes him so hard that he falls into the wall of the circle. "What the…" as the wall lights up and shocks him. Luke walks back to the center of the circle with a scorch mark across his cheek.

"I don't think so asshole!" Christine says as she rides the adrenaline still coursing through her. The smell of burnt flesh in the air. "That's got to hurt!" She gets in fighting stance again.

"That's going to cost you!" Luke says as he throws his hand out with an energy ball.

All Christine does is wave her hands in a, "Bring it on motion". Luke releases it and Christine hits the ground as it goes over her head and gets absorbed by the wall. The circle just swallows it up.

I take off running towards Damon taking him down with a tackle and start punching him in the face. One blow after another. I quickly glance towards Jay and he is in the same position as I am with Storm being the recipient. He has busted her nose. In my head, I am doing the happy dance for him. *You go boy!*

That one quick glance away gave Damon the advantage to throw me off him through the air landing into the wall. *Damn!* I get back up from the ground. I just made the first mistake in any fight. Never take your mind off the target. I look around and see that we, being the good guys are slowly losing control of this fight.

Sirus was getting up from the ground wiping blood from her lip. Phenix has a pretty deep cut on his chin that is flowing freely of blood. Christine is shaking off the effects of Luke who just messed with her mind and he throws an energy ball at Jay which of course he can't see. "Jay!"

He goes flying through the air and hits the ground so hard that he wasn't moving. I was so scared that he was hurt bad. I get down on my knees and shake him gently, "Jay, hey Jay you need to get up." I get no response from him. "Come on Jay, you alright? Hey, no sleeping on the job." I continue to shake his shoulders gently.

He begins to come around and I help him to a sitting position. He gets to his feet a little unsteadily first but gaining his balance. "I guess the fat lady is singing." He looks at me and reaches into his pocket.

CHAPTER 25

J AY STANDS UP AND TRIES to ignore the nasty after taste of the potion he just drank. He shakes off what was left of his nerves and looks around letting out a loud whistle. "Is it always so bright?" He says as he stares in wonder at the glowing circle around us.

"Always." I turn in time to see Luke running towards us.

"Look out!" as I shove Jay behind me because Luke threw another energy ball. I throw my hands up as if to deflect the ball of energy and flames shoot out from them. Luke goes up into flames and explodes and then he is gone. There is nothing but a pile of ash and scorch marks on the ground.

"Whoa!" Jay and I say in union. I shrug my shoulders and shake it off. "I guess the power is tied to my fear." I say. I was scared when I saw that energy ball coming towards us. I was scared for Jay. He is my dear friend and I will not let him go before his time, and that's a fact.

Jay is standing next to me as I point over to Christine. "Hey, she's in trouble, go over and help her out." Jay runs over to her.

She was just getting up from the ground when Jay reached her side and helped her the rest of the way up. Christine reaches up to her mouth and wipes the blood away and looks at him. "Thanks for the hand but you couldn't have come over five minutes earlier?" She tries to smile but ends up wincing in pain due to the cut lip.

"I was kind of in the middle of being unconscious and all, but I'll be sure to get here faster next time." He smiles at her. Just a friendly moment between them in case this was the last interaction they get with each other. Just in case the battle doesn't go in their favor. Christine smiles back understanding exactly what he was doing.

Stephen looked like he was getting the best of Sirus and they run over to her aide. Sirus rolls onto her back and brings her legs up and kicks him in the gut and he goes flying into the wall. There was a static like noise and it lights up like a Christmas tree.

"Damn, that's bright." Jay says causing Christine to stare in shock. "You drank the potion." She laughs and gives him a quick hug. "About freakin time dude." She says smiling.

Jay shrugs his shoulders and says, "Yeah, well when I was flying through the air I heard the fat lady start singing." They reach Sirus who has already recovered quite quickly to her feet.

"What?... I got this." Sirus says as an energy ball hits her lifting her off her feet from the ground.

"Oh, hell no!" Jay says as he takes off running towards Stephen in a charge. He sees this and tries to roll Jay's mind. "I don't think so!" He lands the hit in Stephen's mid-section picking him up like a charging football player. He throws him down onto his back and Jay just starts punching him one after another.

Jay was so lost in his thoughts that he didn't realize that he was still punching Stephen. *His mind was wondering about the potion he took. If Elements added a little something extra to it because he could feel the magick of the circle and of the creatures inside. He remembers Elements telling him that it is permanent. He was thinking just how weird the rest of his life was going to be because of it.* He was so lost he didn't even hear his name being called at first.

"Jay! Jay!" He blinks out of his daze and sees me point down at Stephen. "I don't think he's going anywhere, but Phenix could use a little help." I tell him and he looks at the mess he left on Stephen's face. It was just a bloody pulp all swollen and bleeding freely. He looks over at Phenix and can tell he's frozen.

Jay reaches his side, "Bro what's up?" He says as he waves his hand in front of Phenix's face. He gets no response. He looks over at Elements and shrugs. All of a sudden, a strange sensation runs over his body and he starts looking around. "What the …" and he sees Storm glowing.

Christine is able to break free from it and body slams Storm to the ground. "That's not very cool, bitch." She gets back up and sees Storm not moving. She backs away a little feeling confused. All she remembers thinking when she hit her is that the girl needs to freeze.

I run over to Christine because I can tell she was confused on what happened. "Congratulations girl. You just did your first mind roll." Christine just looks at me as if I were a stranger. "I knew you could do it. You are more like the physic vamps than you realized. Because you are a sensitive."

CHAPTER 26

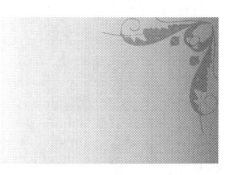

Phenix shakes himself free, "That bitch put a freeze spell on me." He tells Jay as he reaches his side.

"Well she's frozen now on the ground thanks to Christine's mind rolling abilities." They smile at each other.

"Good for her, "Phenix says jumping over Jay's head because he sees Stephen getting up.

Stephen was running straight towards Jay's back. He hits the ground as Phenix jumps over him.

"What the…", Jay looks over his shoulder, "Oh, gotcha. Thanks." Jay gets back up and runs towards them.

Damon throws a psychic blow and it literally hits me in the face leaving a cut. I can feel the warm liquid of blood running down my face as I reach up to wipe it away.

"Is that the best you got?" I say a binding spell to keep him from doing it again.

"Awe, Elements you should know better by now. A simple witch spell will not work on me. My powers have grown since last we met." He flicks his wrist and I find that I can't move.

"Jay!" I yell out before Damon seals my lips. He hears me and runs over knocking Damon down on his butt which cause the spell to break. I feel someone jump on my back and scream.

"You can't do that to him!" Kala yells as she punches my head aimlessly and screams of madness come from her mouth.

"Crap!" I feel more blood stream down my face from the head wound she caused. I flip her over my shoulder and she hits the ground hard.

"Switch with me Jay!" I jump on Damon before he even has time to get up. I see Jay laying into Kala's face making great contact. I glance around quickly and see that everyone is on their last leg. This battle is really taking its toll on us all. I send a small silent prayer, asking for a little more strength to get through this.

Jay knocked the wind out of Kala, lying very still on the ground. "Get out of the way Jay!" I throw my hands out and shoot flames at Kala which consumes her body. All you see is white fire and hear her screams and then she's gone. There is nothing but a pile of ash left the only sign showing she was even there.

"Two down, three to go," I say to Jay who is breathing hard and just happy the bitch is gone. He won't admit it but Kala really did a number on him and caused him some serious pain. I see him limping pretty bad. She must have thrown out his back.

"Don't worry when this is all done I will hook you up with a kick ass healing potion." I smile at him and in return he gives me the evil eye. I just laugh. Hell, that's all you can do at this point.

I may be laughing now but when we get to the end and it is time to do the ritual, there's a good chance I won't be here to even give him that potion. It has been hundreds of years since it was last done and those who performed it, well they didn't make it through.

CHAPTER 27

CHRISTINE IS REALLY DOING A number on Storm. I notice that she has a bruise on her cheek and a nice size gash above her eyebrow. Blood is flowing freely from it running down her left side by the eye. I reach her and ask her to step back and I release flames from my hands and hit Storm which consume her and she is gone with nothing but distant screams echoing the air. Christine falls to the ground totally out of energy.

I bend down to my knees, "Are you alright?" Very concerned for her well-being right now.

She nods her head, "Just give me a minute."

"Jay, stay with her please." I ask and then run over to Phenix.

He is on the ground because Stephen pulled out a knife he kept in his boot. He swipes at Phenix which cut his right side and part of his chest open.

"Noooo!". I reach him trying to help him up.

"Phenix, shift, shift now" I say a freezing spell and direct it at Stephen.

"I can't Elements. If I want to be able to help with the ritual I can't spare the energy on a shift." He says between batches of pain coming from the knife wound.

"Just do a partial, keep your head so that you can speak the words with us." I turn towards Stephen before he can unfreeze and send flames towards him watching them consume his body. I control the flames right into his chest. He is engulfed in white fire and then explodes into a pile of ash.

"You have to do it now Phenix! It's the only way you will begin to heal." He understands and listens to me for the very first time. *Well hell, will wonders never cease!*

I turn all my concentration to Damon. I block out every other sound to where there is nothing but the sound of my heart beat, and breathing which begin to sync together as one. "Gee Damon it looks like your whole team just up and exploded on you." I say in a voice that I don't even recognize as my own. Damon realizes that he is on his own and you can see just a little bit of fear enter his eyes as he looks around.

He can't believe that we being the good guys just took out his whole freakin team. There is nothing but little ash piles scattered about inside the circle. He tries to run out of the circle but my magick is holding steadfast not letting anything out. He is literally trapped like a mouse.

"What do you plan to do?" he says with just enough uncertainty in his voice. "You know your little spells don't work on me. I'm too powerful a vampire for witch's magick." He says with confidence.

The whole-time Damon and I are exchanging words Phenix, Sirus and Christine are getting into their places for the ritual. I look at Christine and give her the signal and then I look at Jay hoping he will understand why it had to be this way.

"Jay…Thanks for everything…Forgive me." With the last being said Christine runs over and shoves Jay outside the circle. Which I release just long enough for him to clear it and then reactivate it within seconds literally, to keep him from getting back in.

"I'm sorry Jay." Christine says with tears in her eyes and barely a whisper.

Phenix and Sirus just exchange looks. I mean they don't really know Jay. He is mine and Christine's friend not theirs. They can see the hurt it is causing us to do this to him knowing this could be the very last time we see him. We may not survive this.

CHAPTER 28

J AY FELL BACKWARDS TO THE ground and gets back up and charges the circle thinking he can break through it. "Noooo!" I hear the charge of the wall as he makes contact and gets thrown back through the air landing on his butt.

I just close my eyes and pray that he will forgive me in time. I look at Damon blocking Jay, and everything else out. No other sound or thought interfering with me and what needs to be done. "Yes Damon, I know my magick has no effect on you. That is why we are doing a ritual that is even older than you are." That's pretty old seeing as Damon is over two hundred and fifty years old. With that you see his eyes go as wide as saucers and if it were possible paler than he already is being a vampire.

"Now!" I yell to my group. Jay is just a mumble of noises in the background. I can't think of him right now so I banish him from my mind. In union and a monotone rhythm, we start the spell.

"Earth, Air, Fire, Water, Earth, Air, Fire, Water, Earth, Air, Fire, Water." We continue this chant over and over bringing our powers to full capacity. I have green light illuminating from me. Red light is coming from Sirus. Blue light is coming from Phenix, and a darker blue light is coming from Christine. These lights represent our elements. They become bright and brighter with each cycle of the words.

Damon's body is starting to smoke like a smothered fire as he feels our power consume him. When our bodies reach its limit and it begins to scream enough, that is when we have to release it and send it straight into Damon.

Our bodies are beginning to burn from the power we are calling up and holding in. All of us are fidgeting as we become uncomfortable holding in the power. It is starting to cause us pain. I give the signal with a nod of my head for the release. All at once we throw our hands up directly aiming towards Damon. A stream of colored lights come from us hitting Damon directly head on and he begins turning into pure white fire.

The color of purity. He opens his mouth and screams. A stream of the white light comes from his mouth shooting up because his head falls back. This tells me the spell is soon coming to an end and so is he. A very loud noise like a bomb goes off and Damon explodes into nothingness. The force of the explosion takes all of us off our feet and sails us through the air sucking out our life's energy and then blackness.

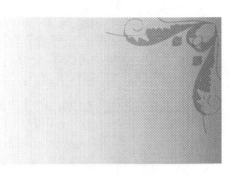

CHAPTER 29

ALL JAY CAN THINK ABOUT is what he saw. He didn't even know that was him yelling in shock. The sky lit up into red flames, blue flames, green flames and lighter blue flames all like a Christmas tree. A loud explosion so deafening to the ear that the force literally knocked you to the ground.

He saw all of them, Phenix, Sirus, Christine, and Elements go flying through the air. They hit the ground so hard that there were indentions to the ground where they landed. He watches them hoping everything is alright. He soon realizes that none of them have moved since they landed.

Jay gets up from the ground and runs towards the circle. Although he could not see it anymore, in his mind he wonders what happened? *Is it over? Did Elements break the circle before she went flying? Why wasn't anyone moving?*

Jay stoops down to Christine and feels for a pulse. It's very slow but it's steady. He makes it over to Sirus who is stirring slightly but has not opened her eyes. He goes over to Phenix, at first, he can't tell if he's breathing. He bends his head lower and puts his ear next to Phenix's mouth and feels a slight breeze on his cheek.

"Dude, I so don't swing that way." Jay jumps back as he sees Phenix open his eyes and chuckles lowly.

"Screw you. I thought you were dead. I was just checking and hoping to make sure." Jay says jokingly but inside he was happy that everyone seems ok so far. He helps Phenix to his feet and they both walk over to where Elements lay.

For once they were linked by the mind. Not by some magickal connection but by something more powerful, Emotions. Both wanting to know if she was alright. Even though neither would say it out loud there is no doubt what they were thinking. *Is she dead?*

They each walk to one side of her and slowly bring their bodies down to the ground on their knees. They both reach out with shaky hands to feel for a pulse. Phenix puts his two fingers to her neck as Jay places two of his fingers on her wrist. They look at each other and their eyes share the same answer... Not even a flutter of movement.

Phenix starts building his energy up to release it into her to shock her heart. It was too soon after the battle to try and build that kind of energy for healing that it just lets out a little spark, like static electricity.

"No, no screw that. It's not ending like this damn it!" He leans her head back to open her air way so that he can begin C.P.R.

"Pull your power in Phenix. It's not helping. Start the chest compressions." Again, a first. Phenix listens and begins the compressions.

Jay didn't care how he sounded, knowing good and well that if Phenix was at his best he could whoop his butt with a flick of power. They both go to work on trying to revive her. Jay blowing breaths into her mouth and Phenix pressing the chest in sequence of three counts.

Jay stops and presses his ear to her mouth... nothing. Phenix starts the compressions again. He counts out loud just to take his mind off the possibility of her being dead.

"Come on Elements." Jay yells at her and blows another breath into her watching her chest rise with it.

"You are not going to let some ass get the best of you, are you?" and he blows another one. The whole time Phenix is doing compressions and trying to bring his mind and heart to terms. *Elements is dead!*

Chapter 30

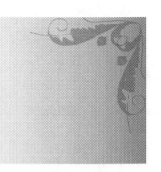

I could feel a warm light hitting my skin. I see white sparkling lights dancing behind my eyelids. In the distance, I can hear a voice.

"Oh child, it is time for you to awaken." The voice is familiar to me yet I can't place it at the same time.

"Can someone please turn down the damn light. My head is pounding." I struggle to open my eyes.

Once again, the voice, but this time it sounds like it's right at my ear and in my head at the same time. "Child, you must watch your language up here."

"What do you mean… Up here?" I say and my eyes fly open. I manage to get to a sitting position and stare opened mouth, "Nan?" Right there in front of me stood my Nan. Well actually floating but still right there.

"What are you….. Ohhhh," I stop myself from finishing the sentence which was going to be, *doing down here?*

I look around and I know the answer. My Nan is not down here, it's more like I'm up there. It dawns on me; *I didn't make it. I'm dead.*

"Nan please tell me everyone is ok. Jay, Christine, Sirus, and Phenix?"

She floats over to me and brushes a hand across my cheek. "Oh, child you always did ramble when you were upset or confused." I smiled at her because she was right.

"Nan please!" I beg of her as I wipe the tears that have fallen down my face.

She takes me into her arms and gives me one of her famous hugs that always made everything instantly ok. "Honey, they are fine. Come I'll show you." She takes my hand and we walk over to what looks like a bird bath, and in it was the clearest water I have ever seen. I mean crystal clear water.

Nan runs her hand over the water and it starts to ripple before it goes still again and an image appears. Well it was more like a movie. I saw Sirus getting up from the ground and then goes over and helps Christine to her feet. The image changes and I see Jay and Phenix. Jay was yelling at me and giving me mouth to mouth. Phenix was doing chest compressions on me. I can hear in their voices that they are scared, and angry all at the same time. I heard Jay say something like, "You can't leave us. You can't leave me."

The image switches back to Sirus and Christine again. I can hear Christine crying and it pulls at my heart and makes me sadder. "Stop it. I don't want to see anymore."

I turn away from the magick bowl, "At least they are all ok and alive." It becomes too emotional and I break down and cry. If that is even possible as a spirit but that is what it feels like to me. This is not how I wanted it to end. This was not how I wanted to say goodbye. I didn't even get to say goodbye or tell them how much they mean to me or I guess meant to me.

My Nan pulls me into her chest again and I just keep crying.

"Shhh, child it's going to be ok. You will see." She rubs my back until my tears have subsided and all that's left are little whimpers.

"Well I guess I'll be able to watch them from up here." I say and start pulling myself together. What's done is done.

"Oh, no child. You have it all wrong. You will not be staying up here." She laughs at me because she sees my expression of surprise and shock. She knew exactly what I was thinking and laughed some more.

"No child you will not be going there either. Besides you do know that there really is no hell, don't you?" I relax a little after hearing that.

"I didn't know for sure. Nan I don't understand. If I'm not staying here or going well never mind, what am I doing?" I am genuinely puzzled and confused.

"Honey you misunderstand this. The only reason you are up here is that the blast from when Damon went boom literally knocked your soul out of your body, and a soul's instinct is to go up when it leaves it vessel."

"I'm not dead? I'm not dead?" and smile crosses my lips and I do my happy dance. I'm laughing and crying all at the same time.

"Well what do I have to do to get back down there? And please don't tell me I have to click my heels three times and say there's no place like home?" I couldn't help myself I just busted out laughing.

My nan is shaking her head at me. "All you have to do is wake up." She says and laughs when she sees my expression.

I give her one more hug because I really do miss them. I can feel my soul start to descend.

I feel a hard pressing on my chest and something brushing my lips. I can hear Jay yelling at me but this time it sounds close.

"Elements you bring your butt back here. Do you hear me?" Jay says and he presses his mouth to mine.

I take a deep breath and start coughing. "Elements, Elements can you hear me?" Jay asks with excitement and has a smile on his face.

Not quite ready to use my full voice I whisper, "Just because I let you kiss me doesn't mean I like you." Jay falls back on his butt and lets out a laugh so full of joy and happiness that I swear he just lost his mind.

"Oh, you bitch, you butthead, I thought you were dead. You are so paying for that." I couldn't help it I start laughing and so does Christine and the rest of them. Jay gets up and starts walking to the house.

Christine screams with joy and falls onto my chest, "Don't you ever do that again! Or I will enslave you and make you my mall buddy."

"Please anything but that!" I put my arms around her for a hug. You see the mall would be my worst nightmare come true. I hate that place. Hell, mall both are four letters. I hate shopping. I would rather clean toilets than go to hell. That's what I call the mall.

Christine wipes tears from her eyes and gives me the biggest smile I've ever seen on her. Sirus just looks at me shaking her head.

"I guess they weren't ready for you up there huh?" That's all I'll get from her showing any kind of concern. She is not big on feelings or girly stuff.

Phenix looks at me closes his eyes and pulls me into his arms and gives me the tightest hug ever imagines. I mean tight. I couldn't breathe. "Hey, bruised ribs here. Can you ease up just a bit?" With that he just squeezes me harder. I can feel him smile into my hair. He helps me up to my feet and we all follow behind Jay.

"Hey speedy, you want to wait up?" Christine says to Jay who pauses and waits for her with his arm out. He puts it around her and they walk together.

We all go into the house and head straight to the kitchen table. We sit down in our usual spots as we start looking at our wounds. Jay being the less hurt out of us walks to the fridge and grabs the beers. He passes them out and takes his seat.

"Here's to kicking ass and still being among the land of the living!" He raises his beer. We all follow suit, "Hell yeah, cheers!" we say in union. We take a big swallow of our beer and just enjoy the taste of it hitting our tongues. I take a deep breath and I look around the table and am grateful we are all able to celebrate. I see everyone doctoring their wounds and nursing the rest of their beer. Life is awesome. *Yee-haw!*